ECSTASY
SORTED
& ON ONE

by

A.D. Atkins

The author would wish to thank and praise the following clubs, organisations and events, some of which he is a member, for their inspiration, assistance and continuing invaluable contributions to the development of the universal language that is house music;

The Final Frontier, Club UK, Universe, The Tribal Gathering, Lost, Cream, Open all Hours @ Ministry of Sound, Eurobeat 2000, Swoon, Mazzo, IT, Heaven, The Cross, Glitterati, Que Pasa @ Bagleys, The Velvet Underground, Pleased, Georgie's, Phoenix and Glastonbury.

All of the aforementioned have a stringent anti drugs policy and have forged close, cogent links with their local police forces and licensing bodies. No inference is intended or should be drawn that illicit drugs have been possessed, consumed or sold with permission or knowledge on their premises. The author is at pains to stress that these clubs actively discourage and disapprove of such activities.

I would strongly recommend that anybody wanting to sample the real verve and fresh innovative spirit of clubbing should visit one of the aforementioned clubs.

Respect to all house music, especially the mesmerising minimalistic beauty of Detroit Techno.

Love and many thanks to all of my friends, clubbers and non clubbers alike, you know who you are!

Printed and bound in Great Britain by the Ipswich Book Company
ISBN 0 9527821 0 3.   Ecstasy, Sorted & On One.
Published by A.D. Atkins.

Mail Order,

A.D.Atkins
P.O. Box 10583
London.
SW1V 3ZL.

Contact tel. 0171 798 8808

Pre Paid Orders. Cheques & P.O.s payable to
A.D.Atkins. @ £9.99 & £2 p&p. Visa and Mastercard
payments to indicate the name and address of the card
holder and the expiry date of the card.

Library Orders

.........Order details for your local library.

Title: **Ecstasy, Sorted & On One**.
Author. A.D. Atkins
Publisher: A.D. Atkins.

ISBN: 0 9527821 0 3

For my wonderful parents, Larry and Margaret
for all their love and support

Volte Face

Volte Face

My gaze was transfixed by the reassuringly solid,
tranquil, early evening skyline that majestically stretched
beyond my living room window. London had loved,
comforted and inspired me for many a year. I'd grown
snug and content in the city that was the centre of my
fascination. I suppose that I'd reached a plateau of sorts,
risks were things which other people took. I'd never
really given it that much thought, not until I got this
phone call, that is. I just sat and listened seeing my
cosseted existence in a completely different light,
watching the same unchanging city skyline that reflected
the very nature of my existence.

"It was the best night ever, absolutely incredible, the
best DJs, the best music, best people, best drugs."
You might have heard that a million times but it was
news to me. I listened transfixed by Tony's enthusiasm.

"You should have seen the sky it was completely
awesome, and the shooting stars, like at about three
o'clock in the morning right, there were these shooting
stars like, loads of them, every three or four minutes.
They blazed a trail across the clear black starlit night.
When I first saw them I thought they were the flares and
the fireworks which we'd let off earlier but no, even the
heavens were taking part in the rave of the year. I've
never had such a buzz you know, it made me feel like I
was at one with the whole world around me. I had three
Es, really good ones, with a Clover imprint on them.
They were just amazing pills, really dancey, buzzy and
everything and everyone seemed just brilliant."

"Sometime in the morning, it must have been a couple of

1

Volte Face

hours after we'd danced as the sun appeared from over the horizon, we did some nose hoovering, Her charlie was incredible, straight off the block, totally uncut. She persuaded me that the perfect way to round things off was to drop a   blotter. Well, it was good for a while and we started to chill on the beach. She got really cold so we left everyone else and went to this cafe like, and I don't know what it was, I could have just been tired or it could have been the two extra blotters she gave me and instead of everything still looking just warm and melty, her face started to crack and get bigger, it got so big that I just had to run out of the cafe screaming but there was no where safe to go, she came after me and held me. I think that I must have slept for a while."

"She says that I just let her hold me but looking the way she did I can't believe that but anyway when it started to wear off and I am talking ages, she tried to give me a couple of pills. Well that was it, even I couldn't cope with more drugs at this stage and I was off, like a shot, down the beach running through what was left of the night befores party hurdling over anything and everyone in sight. She was in close pursuit yelling that she didn't want to give me anymore drugs but that she just thought that I could do with a couple of paracetamol."

"The tripping bit aside and to be quite honest I wouldn't have missed that bit for the world either, it was a real mammoth night. You should have been there. More to the point when I am back in town at the weekend we can go to Whipped and try an E if you like, I don't think that you're quite ready for the trips or anything else but I can

2

guarantee that you'll have a really sound time on a pill, they just make everything all right, give you so much energy and when it comes to dancing well you'll really surprise yourself. Its nothing like going to a sad beer and fight club, this is totally different, bit like when we used to go to Eric's to see the Pistols and all in the seventies there's no pickup atmosphere, just everyone getting in to the music. The real difference though is that nearly everyone there is off their heads."

"You remember that at Eric's people used talk about speed, meth or sulphate or whatever they called it at the time but no actually did it. The communal buzz is like the football where you've got the person next to you talking and you've never met him before like, and you're talking like long lost mates because you've got that something in common, only like when you're partying its like your team has scored all of the time. You've got people just hugging and patting total strangers and when I say everyone, I mean including mega babes you that would normally be totally out of reach. Not that you want to do anything with them, that's the secret I suppose, it represses the sexual drive, hides your ego and increases friendliness and bonhomie. Well I've said enough. It would be really pretty cool though if you could come to Whipped on Saturday. You don't have to join in just come along if you want but I should be able to get some really off your face pills."

I'd listened intensively to Tony's enthusiastic description of last weekend. Well I didn't really know all that much about it but that was then. I know quite a lot more about it now but I really don't know how it all started. I've heard lots of people, and we are talking lots of people talk about their first E but there doesn't seem to be a consensus for consumption and perhaps it would be a little puerile to try to find a common reason. There are after all at a conservative estimate, here in dear old England, out there in our clubs and bars, our house parties, our school discos, our rural and urban areas up to 500,000, people a week who count uncle E amongst their dearest and closet friends. As I say I don't really know how it started but perhaps you'll have a better idea if you hear me out.

"You're only twenty nine, got a lot to learn." I kept repeating the words of the Sex Pistols song. At this age I was supposed to have views on things, to have decided what I was and what I wasn't going to do with my life.

Well I had hadn't I? I had my own flat in the Barbican, I was a Chartered Accountant and a partner, well almost a partner, with one of the top ten firms. I had my close circle of friends. I had girlfriends when I wanted them and could afford more or less what I wanted. There wasn't really that much outside my job which required me making much of a decision, nothing much which required a lot of thought or deliberation, nothing to get me down or concerned apart from all the good causes that I occasionally, doffed my hat to. Like a lot of people I'd made my mind up about drugs. They weren't for me, a couple, come seven or eight pints on a Saturday night but nothing else, certainly not all this white powder we were supposed to do in the financial world. That didn't interest me. Drugs weren't for me. In fact they weren't anything I'd even thought about.

Volte Face

Not until I got that call from Tony that is. I hadn't heard from him in ages. We used to spend a lot of time together at University but only saw him now once or twice a year for a drink. Tony had his own computer software business, specialising in action games, he was always really the creative one. He wanted to know if I'd been out raving. Well of course I hadn't been out raving. Heaven's, I hadn't married but I'd certainly settled down to a fashion. I might have been raving if that's what had been happening ten years ago but no, I hadn't been out raving! He'd told me all about a huge three day beach party he'd been to in North Wales, great music, friendly people, beautiful sunsets, awe inspiring sunrises and that he'd danced all weekend. I hadn't heard him as excited about anything in ages. He wondered if I wanted to try an E with him. Course I didn't. I didn't do drugs did I ?
Well?

Well, I'd heard quite a lot about ecstasy and I'd heard what Tony had to say about ecstasy. A dance with death or the best time you'll ever have with the best people you'll ever be with? It was supposed to help you squeeze the last drop of excitement from a weekend, enjoy everything around you and it wasn't addictive.

"..only twenty nine got a lot to learn.."

"Think about it," he'd said. Well I'd done little else. I thought long and hard. It was going to be my decision, no one elses. It wasn't as if I'd been searching for anything, been in need of anything, not any of those classic reasons for taking drugs. I was curious and rather strangely enough that was sufficient. Besides it sounded bloody good fun and Tony would be there to make sure that everything went well.

It took me four days to return his call but I did and we arranged to meet in Delacey's bar, just round the corner from Whipped where we were going on to. Tony suggested that I should make a bit of an effort dresswise, "none of that Chartered Accountant de rigour weekend wear." He joked, heavens knows what he thought I was going to come dressed as.

Friday of course couldn't come quick enough I'd already decided that this wasn't a drug like any other drug, like heroin, cocaine, amphetamine or even cannabis, this was the alcohol of the nineties, this was what an entire generation took to party, it wasn't addictive, it just made you happy and there wasn't anything to worry about. Period.

I'd been to Delacy's before but that was when it was The Grapes. It had been completely refitted. The jukebox had gone and there was a DJ mixing records on a couple of decks in the corner, all the furniture had gone, replaced by the occasional tidy minimalist table and chair arrangements. Downstairs was more or less empty and I found Tony upstairs sitting at a small round steel table. His tall angular figure leant comfortably and confidently back in the chrome minimalist chair and the harsh overhead lighting shone off his relatively closely cropped dark hair, reflecting off his thick designer spectacle frames. "Alright," we both said in unison, "I'll get you another" I said, pointing at his bottle of Budweiser.

"No it's okay, I am just having the one, you don't want to drink too much because the other stuff dehydrates you as well." Maybe, I thought but I could murder a beer. I got myself a bottle and sat down.

"Well do you want the good news or the bad news?" Tony asked.

I shrugged and he explained that he hadn't been able to get hold of any tablets for the night but he was fairly certain that we'd meet someone he knew who had something. We sat and caught up on old times while the place started to fill up. Tony went round the bar to see who he knew or to see if anybody had anything but to no avail. Not even the girl on the table next to us. She was shuffling and almost dancing in her chair, Tony reckoned she was "on one" already but she said that her friends were waiting to get sorted in the club. She didn't even blink an eyelid when he'd asked her.

I was quite disappointed but Tony reassured me saying that there was normally so much of the stuff around that we'd get something at some stage.

"Let's go to Whipped," he said, "we're better off trying in there." Tony continued to tell me that Whipped was one of the best known and loved clubs in the country, the type of place that people travelled miles to get to and found that their journeys were worthwhile.

The queue was enormous, there were lots of girls wearing 'A' line skirts and long black boots, the boys favouring colourful shirts and checked trousers. I got the distinct impression that the local branch of 'big floppy hats are us' must have sold out. Everyone waited patiently, there was no pushing or shoving, this was a friendly, unreserved and well organised line, occasionally a couple of really glamorous types strolled to the front but they were obviously members or on the guest list. Despite the spirit of bonhomie I was a little uneasy after all it was eleven o'clock on a Friday night, I'd only had the one bottle of Budweiser, I'd no real idea what to expect at Whipped and besides I wanted to go to the toilet pretty urgently. We waited for about half an hour in the queue, paid over ten pounds each and were frisked by a huge bouncer type as we handed back our admission tickets. The search was probably for drugs I thought, well at least there's no chance of them finding anything on me.

"Let's have look around" said Tony, as we moved through into the hot dark, noisy interior. Have a look around, I thought, I can't stop looking around, there were so many people, all of them dancing to the music. Oh yes the music. I wasn't familiar with the music but the beat just picked me up and the solid four-four rhythm reverberated through my stomach.

Tony nudged me in the ribs and shouted against the wall of sound, "look at the way he's standing, he's not moving like everyone else, give us yer tenner,"

I saw a slight youth, with short greased forward hair, no more than seventeen standing by the arches which led to the next dance area. He stood still alone in a sea of perpetual movement, purposely doing nothing but making eye contact with everyone who moved past him.

"Walk past him again", Tony suggested, "he looks like he's doing some."

"Alright," I said, "but you'll have to do the talking, I wouldn't know a diamond or a dove from a dennis the menace."

Volte Face

Tony followed right behind me, I passed the lad in the checked shirt and as I did I heard him mouth one word, just the one word, "pills," I tried to ignore him and walked on a few feet. I turned back and could see Tony talking to him. Well I assumed they were talking to each other. They were both taking, both looking away from each other and both exchanging and examining something in a way so as not to draw attention to themselves.

Tony wasn't gone long, he walked over to me and shouted in my ear, "careful, take hold of this, don't drop it!"
I held the small white tablet in my hand. I don't know what I'd really expected, something bigger, perhaps. "Are you sure, I mean to say it looks like a Panadol to me?"

"Nah, it's about right," Tony confidently replied.

"Hope so," I said with adventurous expectation, concerned that we might have wasted ten quid each, wondering how something reputedly so powerful could come in such a small package.

"Come on," said Tony, "lets do this proper, I'll get some bottled water to down them with, it takes about half an hour, you know."

I went to the bar and got served straight away, I couldn't believe that two small bottles of water cost three pounds but I wasn't too concerned because it was all part of the process, if that's what it cost, well cool, that's what it cost.

Armed with our 33cl bottles of still designer mineral water we made our way to a balcony overlooking the main dance floor. There seemed to be as many people there as down below, most of them already drenched in sweat and dancing. I didn't want to sit down or just stand around, I needed to be seen to be part of what was going on. I started moving to the beats which were coming hard and four to the floor.

"Who's this by?" I asked Tony as the DJ mixed in an awesome tune.

"Papaya New Guinea, it's great isn't it? it's an old one from the Future Sound of London, I'll lend it to you tomorrow if you like. Look, I know you don't need any encouragement," Tony shouted, "It happens quicker if you dance it in,"

"You what?" I shouted hardly having heard what Tony had said. He repeated himself in a jokey mock medical tone stressing that an invigorated circulation assisted the flow of the chemical in the blood stream.

Maybe, but I hadn't even swallowed it yet. No point in hanging around though, here goes, I thought, five minutes past midnight, welcome to a glamorous new experience. I put the whole tablet in my mouth bit it in half and immediately caught an incredibly bitter explosion on my tongue, I instinctively took a mouthful of water and swallowed down. Tony saw my grimace and laughed, "don't worry they're meant to be like that, the chap who's credited with reinventing the stuff swears that you 've got to experience everything it's got to offer, including the taste!" Tony downed his pill and we both started dancing furiously. The adrenaline buzz was amazing, every minute I tried to dance faster desperately trying to detect the first noticeable sign that something was working. Everyone round us was caught up in the music but at the same time there was a great feeling that everyone knew everyone, what I mean is that everyone was smiling and welcoming. I smiled back at everyone, we all cheered together, danced as one, lifted our arms together, we were all friends together. Outside of the club we might have had nothing in common but in there it was pretty obvious straight away that we had a common purpose, to enjoy ourselves and celebrate the incredible music.

After about fifteen minutes I told Tony that I thought it was kicking in. "No," he said, "not yet you'll really know when it does." Despite my protestations he insisted that we left our new friends and put our coats in the cloakroom. "Otherwise you'll just end up a pool of sweat!"

I reluctantly followed him and we tried to make our way through the frenzied main dance floor, there were people just everywhere dancing fierce and furiously, smiling radiantly and having the time of their lives. I carelessly bumped into a lad in a tight black lycra top, he turned round, smiled at me and mouthed in a friendly manner words to the effect, "Alright mate?" I smiled back, he shook my hand and said "have a nice one" as I went past him. It was becoming obvious that everyone was here to enjoy themselves and there was nothing that was going to spoil that.

We put our coats in at a pound a time. Tony explained that he'd look after the cloak tickets in a water proof pouch in his pockets, "otherwise by the time you've danced the night out it'll just be a soggy mess, you're just going to sweat and sweat." We decided to go to the toilets to fill up our already depleted water bottles, agreeing that neither of us was going to pay three pounds for about a half litre of water, no matter where it came from or what minerals it contained. We waited for what seemed an age in the crowded but well ordered toilets. Everyone seemed to have the same idea, they were all filling up their water bottles, washing their faces and some of them were pouring bottles and bottles of water over their heads. The urinals were all but deserted but there was another huge queue for the cubicles. When eventually one of these opened, two lads came out and another two disappeared in. I just looked at Tony with a bemused look. Tony grinned and explained,

"No it's not like that, not that there's anything wrong with that, it's not really that type of place, they're just going in to get sorted or to do billy or charlie."

"What?" I quietly enquired, trying not to be overheard, or to sound too uncool. Tony explained they were either dealing, or sniffing amphetamines or cocaine.

When we came out I was greeted by a very young girl who drunkenly took hold of me and said, "it's my sixteenth birthday and it's my first time, he's going to do it for me, wish me well, kiss me and tell me its alright." I smiled at her boyfriend who was standing impassively behind her. Slightly taken aback I did as she said, and watched her approach Tony in a similar manner before her boyfriend led her into the girls toilets. I got the impression that her novel experience wasn't going to be the same type as mine.

As soon as they left us I wanted to talk to Tony but, no a wave of nausea swept across me, I didn't feel in control any more, I wanted to get off and felt the room spin just like when I'd had too much too drink. What had I let myself in for? I didn't like it and there was nothing I could do about it. "Keep in Control, Keep in Control," I kept repeating to myself as I stood trying not to draw attention to my agony. I'd thought that there was nothing that could possibly go wrong and here I was on my first pill and completely out of my depth, I wished that I hadn't been so stupid, what the hell was I doing playing around with drugs. Somehow I managed to ride the cerebral ferris wheel and stay on, Tony put his hand on my shoulder and said, "It'll be alright," it happens to some people but these are really strong though, perhaps we should have just started off with a half."

Before he'd finished talking the ride was over and I felt a huge wave of euphoria coming over me.

It was alright, I felt alright, well, a lot more than alright, I couldn't express just how alright I felt, I just put my arm round Tony and told him how wonderful I thought he was. He seemed a bit embarrassed but reassuringly patted me back and said,

"Welcome to planet E!"

Planet E, Planet E, Planet E, if this is what Planet E is like well I think I'll stay here I thought! It seemed so right, so much fun. I couldn't remember feeling so relaxed and so happy about everything, everything seemed right and okay.

Tony had a huge grin on his face, he lent across and said, "it's brilliant, just brilliant isn't it! Before we go back dancing though, I know that at the moment you feel that there don't have to be any rules about anything because everything's alright but these are the rules. I should have told you earlier but I think you know most of them anyway. The first is to enjoy yourself. The second is to drink lots of water and the third is to take regular breaks when I tell you to! Last time I came here I forgot to take any breaks, you know unfit I am and after dancing like a mad man for six hours the next week I felt as if I was recovering from the London Marathon."

I heard everything he said, I heard it all so clearly whereas before I'd come up on this stuff it was a struggle to hear anything above the beautiful music. Now everything looked and sounded clearer.

I took it all in and agreed that if he said there had to be rules, well rules there were. Everything was starting to go faster and get better, "I've got to go and dance," I shouted.

"You are dancing!" He laughed.

We moved closer to the dance area itself but there were people dancing everywhere. In the corridors, by the toilets, by the bars and literally on the tables and chairs. Everyone was weaving to the beat that pounded at 130-140 beats per minute. Occasionally the music would stop or slow for five or ten seconds and we were all bathed in a sweeping white light which everyone saluted religiously with their hands in the air palms outstretched.

I was overcome by an infectious, mesmerising, dancing galloping euphoric piano riff, "what's this?" I yelled."

"Le Voie, Le Soliel" by Subliminal Cuts," Tony replied with his arms in the air. "I'm not a great fan of piano music but this is brilliant."

Volte Face

There was no doubt whatsoever I was having a brilliant time. An absolutely brilliant time, I hadn't felt like this before. No never like this before, it was hard to describe, better than making that decisive tackle, scoring that important goal, going out with that special girl. The pile driver crescendos and throbbing beats mesmerised and entranced me. Everyone was my friend and my ego was something which I'd happily left at home. There was a very young lad dancing furiously in front of me, probably sixteen, maybe fifteen, he's got huge big black pupils which seem to have outgrown his corneas and he's wearing a Mr Rush, Mr Man teeshirt. Mr Rush indeed, he certainly wasn't just on the beers tonight. Mr Rush smiles at me, I smile back and its as if we've been friends for life, as we both acknowledge through our dancing exactly how wonderful the feeling is.

Tony dragged me off the dance floor after about two minutes, well it seemed about two minutes but I checked my watch and it was one forty already. We must have been dancing for well over an hour. I was soaking wet and my teeth wouldn't stop grinding.

"Have one of these," Tony passed me a chewing gum, "it'll help your jaws."

We sat down on a slightly raised wall, with our feet off the floor. Within a few seconds we were swinging our feet in rhythm with the music. All of my senses of perception were dramatically increased. Everything that caught my attention was the source of an overly inquisitive fascination. I found myself talking about literally everything that came flooding into my head. I probably sounded like a racing commentator but I

15

recognised a child like innocence come flooding back as my barriers dropped and I had an overriding urge to tell the truth about absolutely everything. It was truly amazing and I felt a cleansing tide, as wave after wave of euphoria swept over me."

"Thanks mate," I said trying hard to elaborate on my understatement, "This is the best fun I've had in ages."

"Yeah, as soon as we hit the dance floor, I don't know, it could have just been the stuff but the music just seemed to get better and better, this place is really kicking tonight." said Tony who was right up there with me.

We filled our water bottles again. I looked at myself in the mirrors and I thought that I looked about ten years younger. Not only did I feel seventeen again I was convinced that I looked it, my skin was radiant and healthy, my eyes were huge. Not even Mr Rush's pupils were as dilated as mine. There was literally none of the cornea to be seen as the black pupils merged with the whites of my eyes. We danced for another two or three hours gradually I noticed that the effect was wearing off, and that the once heaving dance floor was now more sparsely populated, the music was still driving 130-140 beats per minute but it was getting distinctively mellower. Warm and orange is how I think I described it.

We decided to leave just after five o'clock. Just as we were about to leave a large chap in a bandanna and vest came up to me and asked if he could get to the ledge I was standing against. I moved slightly to let him in but that obviously wasn't enough and he repeated himself saying, somewhat apologetically, that he needed a bit more space so that he could snort some lines of coke. I just let him and his friends get on with it.

Outside, I'd never seen anywhere so busy at five o'clock. There were people, cars and taxis all over the place. Everybody looked jaded and drained. Girls wearing clothes the colour and texture of Quality Street wrappers shivered in the crisp morning sun. There was a general air of calm presiding over the sea of sodden shirts and drowned haircuts as groups sat around against the walls chatting, smoking and taking in the early morning breeze which intermittently smelt of cannabis.

Tony asked whether I wanted to go on any where else. I'd love to I thought but not this time, no point over doing it.

We caught separate taxis. Tony was going West.

"Thanks for a great night," I really meant it.

"I'll send you a post card,"

"What!" I laughed,

"Well, tomorrow I'm off to Japan for a month. It's all business but I'm supposed to be going to a full moon beach party, I'll tell you all about it, we'll have to do this again soon."

Lucky sod, I thought and as I was driven off it suddenly dawned on me. I'd have to wait another four weeks to do this again.

I didn't want to go to sleep but I must have because I remember waking up. Perhaps it was the noise of a passing plane, bird song, the postman, I don't know but it wasn't the normal rousing Saturday abdominal pressure caused by a solid nights drinking. I just stretched like a cat and lay gazing at the clear blue sky, watching the little fluffy clouds form and reform high in the atmosphere. I still had an enormous sense of achievement. I wondered what I could do today.

I didn't have to do anything today.

Didn't or couldn't ? I wondered. Moving seemed to be a problem. Not a physical problem. No, I felt that I had a lot of energy. No it wasn't a problem with aching limbs because we'd tried to avoid that last night. No it was a huge weight of apathy, well not a negative depressive apathy but a well "I quite like what I am doing now, I'll think about the other later," type of apathy, rather like last night on the dance floor when I knew I wanted to go to the toilet but it took me about half an hour to actually getting round to doing it ! What ever it was seemed to have me comfortably nailed to the bed.

Brrring, Brrring. The tones startled me at first.

Brring, Brrring, I could get into that tune I laughed at myself, mentally fitting a bass line and four four beat to the tone as I eventually picked the receiver up.

James shouted down the line, "Where were you last night, you missed a real laugh, the boys got pretty steamed up, should have seen Hirsty, one minute he was chatting up this Kiwi girl the next he was being sick all over her, absolute classic."

"Absolutely charming." I retorted.

Well then, were where you? You'd better have a pretty good excuse."

"No, listen," I said, "get yourself round here about five thirty for a game of squash, I had a really good night last night but you'd only laugh if I told you on the 'phone.

Volte Face

"Okay, can't wait," James laughed, with his usual friendly sarcasm.

I eventually got up I couldn't face anything to eat, I had no appetite and besides my jaw still ached a bit from the night before. I drank lots of sugary tea. Normally I hate the stuff but that's all I could manage.

All I did all day was watch Football Focus and catch up on video tape of last nights T.V. highlights.

James came round more or less on schedule. He swaggered in, tall and athletic displaying his customary bravado. " Alright old boy, what's this you've got to tell me then, "

"Well I will if you just calm down a bit, sit down you're disrupting my peace!"

He literally erupted when I told him. I tried to explain the vibe, the feeling but he just kept laughing and mocking. "Druggie, Druggie, Druggie", he baited me persistently. I ended up just laughing with him.

"But seriously have you got any views on E?"

"Well, Claire and her friends are into all of that you know. I did a couple of Es with her last new year when we went to Australia. I haven't bothered since we got back though because she normally does it on a girls night out. You're right they're really good, its just that I couldn't really see you getting into anything like that."

"No, I've surprised myself, very pleasantly surprised myself."

"Perhaps we should go out with Claire and her friends one night, we could try your new wonder drug together," he said, falling about laughing but I knew that he was just as keen as me to drop one.

19

Volte Face

Claire was his German girlfriend, all legs and wonderbras. She was always out and about gate crashing guest lists and monopolising all of the allegedly best parties in town.

"Can she get any pills?" I asked.

"Suppose so, she's always off her head with her mates."

Squash was a disaster, I didn't have the necessary concentration and I literally couldn't be bothered to move for half of even the easy shots that James presented me with. Later we went into Soho to meet some of the boys for a drink. I was still full of my new experience but there was no need to say anything about it, James was already doing that, gleefully recounting a selection of excerpts from my afternoons' recollection. I didn't really mind the barracking, I wasn't in the mood to argue against anything.

A few beers that's all I could manage but that was enough. I didn't feel like getting drunk.

Come Monday morning I felt remarkably bright and fresh. I was buzzing for work. Just five minutes before I get into this, I thought mentally ordering my day with my feet up on my office desk.

"Mr George, it's a Mr Leo Price, line one,

"Thanks." I knew him from when I was training. He'd always kept us amused with his stories of his over active social life. It was all behind him now he reassured us, the wife and children saw to that but it was no bar to having a vicarious social life through the lives of those around him. In the world of accountancy it was refreshing to know someone who wasn't a stuffed shirt.

"Well what's the news then old boy?"

Volte Face

"Oh, no news,"

"How do you mean no news, last time you told me no news, you'd taken up with what's her name, bird with the legs, " he laughed, "are you going to tell me what you've been up to?"

I knew I could trust him. I wondered though if I should test myself to see if I could trust myself not to tell anyone about what I'd been getting up to. Well I could couldn't I? Of course so it wouldn't matter what I told him. It all came out at a gallop a veritable canter of self appraisal and self appreciation. I was proud and I expected his approval.

"Well, my, my, what's brought all of this on I was half hoping for a graphic description of what you got up to with what's her name at the weekend. Any plans to do all of this again?"

"Yes and no, what I really mean is yes its just a case of getting supplies sorted out."

He told me about one of his current trainees, "He's on it, wild boy comes in here on a Monday looking half dead, dies on a Tuesday and only perks up with the sniff of the weekend or a sniff of whatever he's sniffing if you see what I mean. You'll have to watch it old boy, it seems to have a depressive side effect and of course no one knows what it'll have done to you in five or ten years time. That's if you make it that far I wouldn't like to hear about you collapsing dehydrated like a slug with half a pound of salt poured over it. A bright young thing like you doesn't need set backs at work do you."

Not finding him the least patronising I explained that I felt totally in control. "I feel fine, better than normal actually I'm two hangovers down and I can still feel the adrenaline pumping."

"I see but don't say I didn't tell you so. Hah hah! Now tell me about young so and so, how's she?"

I wasn't too sure who he was referring to. Not that I had strings of girlfriends, heaven forbid. It was just that I hadn't spoken to him for a while and quite frankly I couldn't remember who we'd talked about last. There was no one special at the moment.

"Nothing to tell," I yawned, haven't seen her for weeks, can't be bothered, other more important things on my mind. Why, do you want her number?"

"Oh no, no, no No! I don't think so, wouldn't be wise would it, a happily married man like me. I'll leave that to you younger boys. Anything else on the horizon?"

"No, I yawned again."

"By the way you haven't told anyone else about your experience have you?"

"No!"

"Well, don't. We have to strive to keep up a professional image that borders on the mind numbingly boring. Excitement is bad for business, joking besides you've got that partnership to think about."

"yeah thanks," I said,

"Well, toodle pip."

"Bye."

Positive Education

The dust kicked above me as I clattered to the hard, sun dried earth. Another long summer had taken its toll on the once lush playing field. I lay for a while gazing at the distant elms. The tall, mature trees loomed over me. Broody and mystical, they reached to the greying firmament. The fall had been caused by my lack of commitment, not the malice of my opponent. It was just as well that there wasn't enough time to restart the game. It had been one of those matches, I'd sliced every shot, under hit passes, mistimed my tackles, moaned non-stop, shouted at everybody. I'd blamed anyone but myself and generally got on the nerves of my team mates. My mouth was dry from the taste of the dust, the culminative dehydration of the weekends clubbing and the demands of playing five aside in the evening sun. As I hobbled out of the park I effortlessly gupled down a two litre bottle of water and a can of diet coke. We were going to the pub but I needed to hydrate first, I didn't really have an appetite for beer.

James and I enthusiastically discussed clubbing in the pub. I was amazed at how quickly I was getting into it all and I think we were both grateful for our common interest. Perhaps it's right what they say about drug users being the most boring people in the world. All they talk about is themselves and their drugs. A crowd of James' fiancee's friends were going clubbing at the weekend. Pretty glamorous girls and fun with it, he announced. As if I needed any further incentive. Even better they'd got good supplies, no need to worry about where my next E was coming from. We'd all meet at his house and go on from there. There was no point in meeting in a pub, it was all too much effort and anyway they closed at eleven o'clock.

James shared a modest, West End, top floor stucco flat with Claire and Greg. The stairs up the five floors provided a healthy challenge. I didn't trust the lift which seemed to break down at least once a week. There was no way that I was going to be stuck in a lift shaft when all of my friends were going out on E. As James opened the door, my deep breaths meant that I caught a mouthful of stale cigarette smoke. It wrenched with my empty stomach. We exchanged greetings and ambled inside, James slid open the balcony windows at my request.

Greg's considerable bulk was slouched on the sofa, beer in one hand, a fag in the other. A takeaway pizza box was balanced precariously on his stomach. He was totally engrossed in an action film which blared out from the television.

There was no sign of Claire or her friends.

"Seen, it before?" Greg enthused, "It goes absolutely ballistic in a couple of minutes, get yourself a beer and get ready to see Arnie give it loads."

Well I wasn't too interested in Arnie or anyone else giving it loads quite frankly.

"Where's Claire?" I enquired.

"Oh! She's gone to some party with her mates."

Positive Education

"What!" I felt immediately deflated. I noticed boys weren't dressed for going out, lounging around on the sofas they weren't going to move tonight.

"Sue couldn't get any, not a lot around at the moment, besides she says the last stuff she got was crap!"

"What about tonight then?" I asked feeling totally dejected.

"We could just go for a drink then, Greg's found this working men's club just the other side of Paddington that's open all hours" said James

"You must be joking I've been waiting all week for this!"

James smiled playfully, I could tell that he was keen to go.

"Shut up druggie!" sighed a subdued Greg.

Saturday night was normally his one night of recuperation after a hard weeks solid drinking

"I'll watch the end of the film and come out with you but they better serve beer, I am not going to be drinking bottles of poxy water all night long."

At least that sounded a bit more promising. Come the end of the film though, the two of them took for ever to get changed and dressed. Calling a cab took even longer but eventually we set off to party, James decided that we'd catch some hard trance and techno at what he described as the best club in town.

There was something special about whizzing through the London streets in the early hours of the morning. Speed limits and traffic lights only seemed to matter where they were enforced by police cameras. Our driver, a tall sheep coated Moroccan, with large side burns growing from underneath his furry Cossacks style hat, occasionally turned round giving us enigmatic grins. It was as if he knew what we were going out for.

The queue looked at least an hours worth. The club was absolutely road blocked. One o'clock in the morning and it snaked round the corner and past the car park. We decided to wait, there was no way that I was going home.

"Listen," said James, "truth is, these days you don't know what you're getting drug wise, could be ecstasy, speed, caffeine, ketamine, ephedrine, could be nothing. We've just got to try to find someone with some good stuff. Won't be easy to find. Best way is to ask someone who's dancing mental, people don't mind being friendly, they've probably been in the same situation themselves. Leave it to me I'll get us sorted tonight."

Inside the club James went off on his own mission in the direction of the toilets, while we stocked up on bottles of water and put our coats in the cloakroom.

The club was huge, totally kicking and absolutely packed. There were three main areas, a large ballroom with lots of satellite seating areas, another large, darker room boasting solid banging bass drum beats punctuated by hissing synthesised open snare drums and the occasional burst of white light. The third room was much smaller and had a much more intimate sort of party atmosphere to it.

James met up with us on the edge of the first area. He stood out towering above the gyrating mass.

"Nothing!" He said. I got a couple off blokes trying to sell me stuff but I don't know, I just got the impression they were too keen, the tablets had fracture lines and doves but then again anyone with access to a pill press can make a tablet with a dove on it these days. You've really got to watch out for snide Es, I've even heard about dickheads selling on one hundred per cent plaster of Paris as ecstasy."

We decided we'd look around the club, check out the atmosphere. All three rooms were going absolutely wild. At the back of the main room we dropped down some stairs and right back up again on the other side. A tall, older looking lad, perhaps just younger than ourselves tersely said "pills" as we passed. James dropped back and took the bait. I saw James hand the lad money. He checked it and passed it to a girl sitting on the balcony rail. Just as he did Greg started to talk to the lad.

Oh! no, I thought that's blown it. They want to be discrete and now we've got Greg butting in. I tried to melt away but it became increasingly clear that Greg and the lad were getting on, no problem. I waited until Greg pulled me over.

We said hello and exchanged names. My mate the dealer said he was called Steve. He introduced me to the girl on the balcony. That was Jules, his girlfriend.

These were fourteen quid. James said this was more of a going rate for a club. Three quid from manufacturers six to eight from middle range dealer eight to twelve in the street and ten to fifteen in most clubs. It was pretty obvious that there was a lot of money to be made and that the market price reflected more what the punter had to spend on a night out than what he was actually buying. These things cost nothing to make, it was the old power equals knowledge equation.

Positive Education

Steve seemed friendly enough but I was a little wary of talking too much to him, after all he could have just fleeced us to the tune of fourty two quid. At least before we moved off to dance he told us he'd still be there for most of the night and we'd find him dancing in the back room if he sold out.

This time I didn't come up so violently. Whilst the pills were just as bitter the effect was much smoother and with none of the room spinning or panic. In fact Greg and James agreed that they'd come up gently after about forty minutes. We danced together and Greg in particular seemed to be reliving a youth passed by, I certainly didn't hear him complaining about not being able to drink beer. Later on I went back to see Steve. I wanted to congratulate him on his product. He was still there dealing but Jules had gone off. "She's on one," he said, "well loved up." Apparently Jules helped him out, she kept the cash and he had the pills when they were dealing so that he couldn't be caught with both at the same time. Steve called his pills yellow callies, saying they were some of the best stuff he'd had in ages.

"I was down the pub with my mates last Sunday and they put two in my beer, don't know how I got home or to work the next day all I remember is driving like a mad man rolling my head and eyes round and sort of puffing my mouth out and gurning when ever someone told me to look where I was going." I began to take a genuine liking to Steve, he was immediately friendly, a solid to the point bloke, a million miles away from the stereotype I had of a shifty two faced dealer selling dodgy goods with a gun in his back pocket.

Positive Education

We just sat and chatted for an age, he didn't seem to be bothered about not being able to put out his sales pitch and I didn't seem to be bothered about what I told him about myself, who I was, what I did, where I lived. Things that given who and where I was, I should have kept to myself. It was probably the stuff, it just seemed to open me up, there was no way I could say something which wasn't true no way that I could put a opaque glaze on it. Steve told me he lived on the coast, worked with cars. He regularly tried to deal here to supplement his meagre earnings, he knew though that if the bouncers or the management got wise to it he'd be handed straight to the Police. Like most of the clubs, this place had stringent procedures to keep drugs out of their club but given the size of the tablets, nothing short of fully strip searching all their customers could stop or deter the really determined.

Steve said, "Have a half with me its four thirty and I want to unwind for a bit before I drive back home. Don't worry it'll just keep you going for a bit longer."

He was right and when the lights came on at just after six am. We all kept right on dancing, still being propelled at full throttle. It was in a direct contrast to an alcohol party where everyone stops what they're doing when the lights come on and starts nosily complaining. Here everyone cheered. Everyone was looking at and talking to literally anyone who caught their eye.

James and Greg were still buzzing. What they hadn't told me was that they'd each taken another one half way through the night. With their ear to ear grins. They described, just what great times they'd had and what should we do now? Good question I wanted to go out, to go on somewhere to do something else but I wanted to keep all of this in proportion. I don't know why but there was some part of me which wanted to go home and read the weekend papers or something as equally lazy or silly. A lot of people seemed to be going on to the Leisure Lounge, SilverFish, Trade and wherever. The licensing laws seemed to have banned open air raving and decanted it into a plethora of clubs running at all imaginable hours. It was possible to club non stop all week in London, there was literally somewhere every night and day of the week.

Greg's imagination was running riot, "There's no need to go home! Ever! No need to go home ever these places are open all the time, whey hey I've moved out already!" he exclaimed. I dropped out and got the taxi as far as my house. I couldn't really see them going on.

Come Monday I felt a dose of the flu setting in. I was pretty tired but I wanted to know what I could find but about this stuff, it had really excited my curiosity. Where could I start though? Hardly the type of thing I'd find columns on in the local library after all its only been on the scene for the last ten years. I remembered then where I'd first read about it. It was in my copies of The Face. I'd never cancelled my subscription and I kept them filed in and on a bedroom shelf

I pulled out a pile which must have gone back ten years and began wading through them cover first. Yes it would be on the cover I realised as I took in the pictures of the glitterati that graced the covers. Some of the copies were familiar, friends from the past others, unread, possibly unopened.

Undeterred by the dust I paused, reading the occasional snippet. I found several articles ranging from stories of how the drug first appeared on these shores, how it was used in large amounts by the revellers who'd turned Ibiza into one large club for most of the summer. Stories of how to spot an ecstasy user. You want to know how? Well apparently they never sleep, drink copious amounts of soft drinks or water, hardly eat and well, wait for it, like to hoard and cuddle up to lots of pastel pink and blue teddy bears. The magazine humorously recommended that you check out your younger sisters bedroom for these signs.

I'd nearly got to the end when wow, as if by magic here it was, what I'd been looking for, the story of Alexandra 'Sascha' Shulgin. "The Stepfather of Ecstasy"

It was quite a long article but by the time I'd finished reading it I knew that I had to buy his book. Here was a man with a level head on his shoulders telling the world about his twin loves, his wife and the chemicals he'd discovered, rediscovered and tried with a religious relish. It also promised an insight into the chemical make up of ecstasy and how to make it.

I just had to have it. The American 'phone number suggested that I try their English distributors. I did and the chap said that he'd ship it to me straight away and that it should be with me tomorrow.

I couldn't wait.

Positive Education

Next morning I decided to take the day off. The weekend had really taken its toll this time and I was over tired and full of flu, cold or something.

"Its the flu you see, can't really do anything justice unless I give it a day of under the covers" I said truthfully as I rang into work.

"Are you sure, you know that we've got to get the Welsh job done by Friday"

Yeah, you know me, this must be my first sick day in three years."

"Okay but give me a ring this afternoon." said Middlehurst, my manager, he was a steady friendly sort of bloke not adverse to a bit of partying himself but definitely not the right person to tell about this type of partying.

There was a special type buzz about being at home when I should have been at work. I loved my work but it felt like a real bonus to have some extra time to myself once in a while. I suppose I didn't really expect my book in the post today, but sure enough it arrived, before nine am as well. A Chemical Love Story" by Alexandra Shulgin. It was divided into two halves one dealing with a life/love story, the second a chemical love story detailing the recipes for 198 or so psychedelic amphetamines

'3,4 Methylene-dioxy-N-Methyl-amphetamine,' MDMA that's what I was interested, in Methelynedioxymethampethamine - Ecstasy! Phew!
I'd never seen so many chemical names, compounds or processes in my life. I read it religiously. Surely it must be possible to make this stuff. I didn't know my

penathelenye from my allybenzene but I was convinced that it was possible.

I spent all day reading. I forgot to ring work. I forgot to cancel football. I can't remember eating. Somehow despite my cold, the book carried me through the day and the early evening.

I was slightly thrown and startled when the telephone went. I looked up and realised for the first time that the sun had receded far over the horizon and that the calm summer sky was lit only by the quarter crescent moon and distant stars.

"Where were you when we played football ? Where the hell have you been, it was five against four dickhead, the least you could have done was to ring so I could have made the numbers up. We're in the Mitre and I'll expect to see you in fifteen minutes."

James had meant it in a joking sort of way I had let them down. I was about to say that I'd be there as soon as possible but he'd already put his mobile down. I'd completely lost any idea of the time but it was ten thirty when I checked.

I thought that I'd better get out at least and see the outside of the flat once today. I pulled a pair of jeans on over my shorts grabbed my new bible and ran out in the direction of the pub. I got the usual barracking reserved for anyone who was late. Ironically most of the boys left soon after eleven o'clock but this left me with the opportunity to talk to James, Lewis and Graham alone.

James laughed when he read the dust jacket of my new book. He didn't believe me when I told him that I was seriously suggesting that we made the stuff.

Positive Education

"There's the legal side to think of, you could get life for that you know?" He laughed dismissively, "you'd never get all of the materials. I've heard that part of the process uses so much heat that it can be picked up on satellite and never mind the police what about all the other low life making this stuff it's hardly a market regulated by the normal rules of competition, tread on someone's feet here and you'll have something real to worry about."

Graham broke his silence, he looked pensive and said, "Well I don't know you can make anything if you start from carbon, might take some time though." he joked. "No seriously," he said, "I've heard that botanical synthesis is the answer to all of the government imposed hurdles when it comes to making this stuff. I've got a degree in organic chemistry and from what I can gather most substances like this have a similar chemical make up and most of the materials needed to start the process can be found in plants."

"That's cool," I said, "I've read about nutmeg and sassafrass in here."

"Yeah, most of the plants producing essential oils will get you there sooner or later, the two plants you've mentioned and calamus are the big ones. It's not a five minute job though, other wise you'd have everyone making it, there'd be none of these weekend gambles hoping that what you'd buy was actually going to do something. No, if it was that easy then everyone would be making it, everyone would have their own junior chemistry set and their own guaranteed supply." Lewis agreed, I knew that he'd also got a chemistry degree.

"And be risking huge jail sentences," I added

34

Positive Education

"Yeah but the chances of getting caught are relatively small on the manufacture side I think it would be fun to have a go, if I didn't have the wife to think of," said Graham

We didn't talk about it for too long after all we all had work the next day. I was the only sober one of us all and despite my reservations about the legality of it all I was pretty keen to have a go. I wasn't sure about the others. I read some more of the book before realising. That I'd have to get some sleep at some stage.

The brilliant early morning eastern sun always flooded through my curtianless, tower block, windows waking me literally at the crack of dawn. Not today though, it was eight forty am. Damm, I'd overslept again but there was no way that I could miss work two days on the run. In any event I was quite missing it after a days absence. I should have been there an hour ago and felt an uncomfortable panic set about me as the shock of seeing the time on the clock. I was behind schedule, I hated that feeling, that whatever you did in the day that you'd never catch up with what you should be doing.

I forgot to have a shower in my determined haste to get where I should have been. To make matters worse my head was full of cold and a dank dark wave of emotion flashed across me as I'd left the building aware that I'd splashed cold water across my face but forgot to have my all essential pint of water. I bought a can of diet coke and a bottle of evian water at the tube station. This put me back on course but as I got to the bottom of the elevator I cursed myself as the tube thundered out of the station. I had to wait a whole three minutes for the next one . It put me in a foul mood for the rest of the day. My head was full of phenalthetamines and amphetamines but today it didn't really matter. I hadn't finished the book. Should I have put it in my bag? Of course not. I couldn't have read it on the tube, certainly not in the office.

I pushed myself on to the tube somewhat surprised at my own rudeness. I sifted through the mornings post which I'd managed to grab on the way out. All of the usual stuff, ACA. News, Bank statements, credit card statements and right at the bottom of the pile a post card from Tony. Postmarked Kyoto and with a scene of coastal bliss on the front it, read;

Dear Jerry,

Whipped was great, glad you seemed to have enjoyed it. Japan is fascinating and I'll tell you all when I'm back. In the meantime go shopping. Try these; Future Sound of London, 'I.S.D.N.'; Underworld.... anything!!!; DJ. Misjah & DJ. Tim 'Access', Cream 'Live',; There's a real selection there. Most shops will have them but if you've got any problems try Fat Cat in Soho. Good shows to listen to are Kiss FM, anytime but best on Tues., Thurs., Fri. & Sat. evenings, Radio 1 Fri. & Sat evenings. Set your video for BPM. on Sun mornings.

Look forward to another big night, will ring you when I get back.

Enjoy Tony!!

Positive Education

At least that put me in a bit of a better mood. It was good of him to let me know all of that,   after all I hadn't bought a decent record in ages.   Heavens, 'Pump up the Volume' by Marrs,   'Love Can't Turn Around' by Jack Master Farley Funk and a few records by The Orb and The KLF must be the last things I'd bought. I didn't like the indie bands which hadn't really changed at all in the last twenty years or the Beatles copyists who were breaking the hearts of young girls and boys alike. I remember thinking back and regretting that I'd thought I was far too old to be dancing in a field somewhere off the M25, I should have known better. Realistically for me the last five years had been a bit of a musical oasis, bereft of the awesome tunes that I'd been hearing in these marvellous clubs.

The first thing I noticed when I went into one of the large shops was that there wasn't a piece of vinyl in sight. I spent ages looking for what I wanted. I didn't want to ask, that wouldn't be cool, even if the records I was going to buy were cool.

Well I had to in the end. I realised that the problem was that I was looking in the Rock and Pop section where I'd always found what I'd needed in the past but all of what I wanted now was in the Soul and Dance section.

It was all there apart from DJ Misjah and DJ Tim. I later concluded to myself that this must have been someone's way of saving the best for last. On the way out of the shop I saw a display in the book department headed in large letters "Drugs". That deserved a closer look. There were piles of books mainly on how to grow your own marijuana, how to do it in a council house, how

37

to do it with special lights, how to grow the strongest varieties. Books on the secrets of LSD, psychedelic experiences, magic mushrooms, laughing gas, poppers, prozac, opium use and then I saw what I'd really been looking for, copies of 'Phikal' by Alexander Shulgin and 'Ecstasy and the Dance Culture' by Nicholas Saunders. The former I was happily familiar with and the latters cover comprised of a large silver E which shimmied under the store lights. I flicked through it amazed and enthralled by the depth of information it contained. I must have spent an absolute age in there, I checked out literally everything on the shelves, taking on board a wealth of information, there were even books on legal highs drawing on the effects of plants, berries and nuts which had been used down the ages for all manner of purposes to change conciousness.

My consciousness felt it was being expanded just by reading these pamphlets from heaven. Chew khat for a speedy effect, snort ephedrine for similar results. Kola nuts, kava kava or nutmeg oil gave a warm empathetic effect similar to the mellow effect of E. Magic mushrooms for a high and the giggles.

I eventually bought Nicholas Saunders book, a copy of the Secrets of Methampethamine Manufacture by Uncle Fester, surely not his real name and a pamphlet about Magic Mushrooms. I decided that Uncle Fester had got it about right, whilst it might be just about legal to read and write about these things it surely wasn't going to be that smart to leave my credit card details. Especially if one of the books was about production of the stuff.

Positive Education

Luckily I had enough cash on me to pay there and then. I thought that I might as well kill two birds with one stone. I picked an assistant who looked as if he might know. He had long hair tied back, a boot lace tied around his neck and a Bush records teeshirt.

"Do you know where Fat Cat Records is mate."

"Yeah, Yeah, round Seven Dials, it's Earlham Street I think, you're best asking when you get down there 'cos my directions are hopeless."

I paid the man, thanked him for his help and dashed in the general direction of Soho and Covent Garden. I wanted to get there and get home as soon as possible, I had books to read for heavens sake.

Dam. I couldn't find Fat Cat anywhere. Everytime I took one of the roads, and if you know Seven Dials you'll know just how many roads there are, off the seven Dials roundabout, resplendent with its eponymous obelisk. All I got from the people I asked was either, "well, I think it's round the corner," or, "where?" Great obelisk I thought to myself, great bloody obelisk but I don't want to spend all afternoon looking at it. At least the tour around the Seven Dials was of some educational value. It seemed to be the heart of the periphery of Club culture. The Ministry of Sound had a shop there, so did Sign of the Times, there were other record shops all equally as good no doubt but it was this particular one I needed to find and I wasn't going to stop now.

It seemed an absolute age had passed before I stumbled on a sandwich board opposite a radiant flower stall selling enormous sunflowers, huge pieces of moss covered branches and flowers so exotic that I hadn't seen before let alone had half an idea as to what they were. The sandwich board was the clue I'd been looking for. It said 'Fat Cat Records downstairs'. I must have passed it several times before but it was only now that I realised I'd been looking for a shop window but that Fat Cat was downstairs beneath a Clothes shop.

I followed the signs, down the stairs past an illuminated fluorescent painting and I was hit by the throb of funky hard underground acid. I also immediately realised why no one outside knew where Fat Cat was because all of those imparted with the knowledge seemed to have wedged themselves into the shop itself. It was absolutely heaving. Full of a club type of punter typically aged eighteen to twenty five, mainly but not exclusively male. Most of them wore their hair short, not aggressively short but fashioned in a seemingly unfashioned way to a similar length to that of the goatee or side burns which were occasionally sported. There were a plethora of tee-shirts emblazoning record label names and logos, "old school", 1970's style trainers in canvas and rubber escaping the high-tech development of running shoes as a sports phenomenon and accepting them for what they are, namely, a cheap comfortable vehicle for walking and loafing around in.

The walls of the small shop were racked with alternative dance sounds in all formats. But it was mainly vinyl. The wall behind the serving area groaned under the weight of twelve inch singles which were racked like magazines, the staff seemed to be constantly handing down large numbers of these items to the customers in the shop.

Positive Education

A row of professional turn tables was surrounded by a group of serious looking young men. Their heads were bowed, ears hidden by large headphones and they looked intensely down at the vinyl which they were spinning on the Technics SL1200s. A note above the record decks read that all cartridges had to be returned with the records loaned and that there was to be a charge akin to the cost of a replacement stylus if it was not returned. No one was going to risk being ostracised here by pinching a cartridge, it was more of a club than a shop.

I was the only person in a suit but it didn't seem to matter this wasn't the type of place where someone was going to laugh at you for wearing last weeks tee-shirt, last months trainers or listened to music they didn't approve of. There wasn't a holier than thou attitude pervading the place, just the happy diligent ambience I'd noticed in Whipped. it was almost a spiritual type of thing though I am sure that they'd laugh if you suggested that to them. No, as I was later to find out that type of thing was for the Goa trance gurus.

I moved my way to the counter and must have stood there for an age as the staff continued to exchange brief warm friendly banter whilst passing down records. The boy standing next to me handed back up a pile of records. The assistant totalled them up on a calculator, and said, "£84.70 please."

£84.70 for a pile of no more than a dozen twelve inch records. The customer didn't look old enough to work never mind old enough to have a spare £80 or £90 a week spare to spend on records. He didn't look the type to go stealing to fund his hobby. I was literally flabbergasted. He just handed over the cash exchanged pleasantries again and left.

"Be with you in a second" the short young lad with cropped hair behind the counter told me as he handed down another batch of records. He was wearing a black in house tee-shirt with a small logo of a Fat Cat, probably a tom, on all fours with a fat electrocuted tail. Cool logo, far better than all of this cheesy futuristic space junk recycled for the umpteenth time from the sixties and seventies.

"What can I get for you? "he asked after a few minutes.

"What's this playing?" I asked as I listened to a massive hard, funky acid track.

"Winx and Conciouness, it's a Strictly Rhythm import."

"I'll take that, DJ Misjah and DJ Tim's "Access" and a few others like them, I'll trust your judgement," I said hopeful of taking home an armful of wicked tunes.

"Try these," he said pointing me to the direction of the decks.

"No it's alright I'll just take them."

I handed them back to him one by one. Awacs "It's our future." Heller and Farley, "Extra Flava" "Rythim is Rythim, Strings of Life", Dave Clark "Red Three," Hardfloor "Acperience" Hardfloor, again this time "Mahogany Roots" and Green Velvet's " Cameras Ready Prepare to Flash."

Just over £50 that wasn't too bad and I could take them back if they weren't to my newly acquired tastes.

I was a little reluctant to leave the mesmerising whirl that was the hidden secret of Fat Cat. When I did get back outside I suddenly remembered my urgency to get back home. I had books to read and music to soak up. I didn't know which to do first so I sat there blasting myself out with these remarkable records and fascinating literature.

I put the Gaggia Machine on the plate glass table in the lounge, sat in my home made Frank Gherry derived cardboard chair. I'd made it myself from a photo in one of the Sunday Supplements, it was simple enough, just rolled corrugated cardboard held together in the shape of a traditional arm chair. It was remarkably comfortable. It needed to be, I don't remember going to bed that night, my adrenaline pumped, I had the urgency about me that I recalled from marathon exam revision stints but this was much more fun and I was learning so much about life and how to access previously unexplored areas.

Pages turned, veins throbbed and my heart and spirit raced with the regular boost of caffeine and the four four beat that belted out of the speakers at anything from 120-140 BPM.

The evening raced by and the morning approached with the glorious rise of the suns fearsome fiery furnace. I still hadn't finished the book and it was nearly time to think about going to work. Sleep wasn't a good idea. I settled for a shower instead.

I had to go to work but today my heart was with the secrets of methampethamine manufacture. I even thought about taking the books with me to read in a quiet moment at work. I had my own office and to an extent dictated who came into it and when. No, I told myself there was no credible way I could explain these books if someone found them. It just wasn't worth it and besides I had work to do. I might have been able to do two things at once at home but work was different there was a lot riding on it, not just my professional future but the interests of the company and it's clients. I'd have to be careful about keeping my professional and social lives separate, it was never right to mix the two.

Despite my night shift I felt remarkably refreshed at work that morning . I was in control and enjoying what I was doing something was making me very happy. More than that I was learning ways of maximising that happiness. To try to stay up on E, a few lines of speed helped and Vicks inhalers apparently gave a gentle buzz that was similar but not as strong as poppers. Vigorous dancing and the encouragement and attention of friends on the dance floor helped, so did smart drinks and standing on your head. To help getting up there in the first place it was best to have an empty stomach. Some people found that being quiet and still helped promote coming up high and well and reduced the risks of anxiety as to the strength and purity of the tablet. Others preferred vigorous dancing to come up. What was apparent though was that in order to get the best out of E you should do it with friends. It wasn't something to be taken at home by yourself. There was an entire culture out there and I wanted to know as much as possible about it.

I felt invigorated, refreshed, rejuvenated and utterly and completely, one hundred per cent in love.

Train of Thought

From what I'd gathered it was quite easy to make E. I wanted to have a go but I wasn't going to be able to do it all by myself. If I was going to go through with it I'd already made the mistake of telling people that I was getting into the stuff. One of the biggest rules when you want to do something against the grain, something not quite right or whatever is to keep it to yourself. Not to impart the information to anyone who doesn't need to know it. Bragging and showing off is a sure way to get caught. Someone will always tell the wrong person, normally out of ignorance sometimes out of spite. It was best to keep it to yourself.

Most of my friends had as much to lose as I did if it all went wrong, they were all professional men. At least if it went well there shouldn't be too much to worry about. If it went wrong then that was something I didn't even want to think about. I needed to have responsible partners who wouldn't crack and give the game away.

I could forget about Graham, he'd said as much in the club, he was married and would probably have to tell his wife at least something about it. Pity though because his scientific knowledge would have been a real bonus. No, switching off my P.C., I realised that there were only two ideal candidates and I'd need them both. I slipped out of the building, past the security guards and over the polished marble floor of the grand atrium entrance. I picked up lunch at Pret A Manger.

Train of Thought

Hum, Bacon, and Avocado Salad on tomato and walnut bread, Chocolate brownie, wild flower, wild fungi and nut salad and a couple of bananas. Since I'd been taking E there was always one day of the week when I went really food mad. It was normally Monday or Tuesday. I suppose that a pattern was emerging. Friday I hardly ate anything because of the adrenaline rush associated with going out and the need to make sure that my stomach was empty enough for my pill to have its full effect. Saturday was similar eating more or less depended on whether I was going out or not. Come early evening on Sunday I had normally worked up a bit of an appetite. I noticed that I was eating less than normal most days. To compensate I pumped myself full of Vitamin C, B, B6, B12 and amino acids like Tyrosine and Trytophane which were supposed to be depleted by a hard nights dancing. I mercilessly consumed ship loads of bananas and even tried a body building drink called Ultimate Orange which as well as replacing essential vitamins and minerals contained herbs and plant extracts which gave it a mild legal stimulative effect.

I planned to just walk for half an hour or so, just to take in the fascination of the City, watch the crowds as they drifted and hurried through the busy narrow lunch time streets. I wanted to have some space in the frenzy around me to formulate my ideas. Well that was what I'd planned to do but I couldn't leave it any longer, I needed to talk to the boys about ecstasy. I'd use a public call box. Far better than dialling from work or my mobile. I rang James and Lewis. I couldn't say much in case the lines were taped. They often were, to guard against insider dealings and sharp practice in the City institutions. English Oil International for one wouldn't take too kindly to the stock shrinkage I was planning or the fact that the equipment their shareholders had paid for was going to go into drugs production.

James was going to have to be in on it all. There is no way that I could have hidden this from his natural curiosity and child like spirit of adventure. It would be far better to have him there and in on it. He'd be able to brighten up those long anxious hours.

Without Graham, Lewis was going to be essential. More to the point he'd fill two roles, chemist and quartermaster. Lewis was my direct means of access to licensed and proscribed chemicals and glassware. High Streets were changing, they no longer contained shops which sold chemicals over the counter. The only things that we could get over the counter were the essential oils sold in herbalist and occultist shops and even these were being restricted by prohibitive price and poor supply. Homogenisation of retail outlets and the strict laws governing the supply of items which may be associated with the drugs trade had seen to that. I often wondered where other manufacturers got their supplies from, other people like Lewis? From abroad or from rogue suppliers? It didn't really matter. At least from what I could gather we had our source ready to tap.

James and Lewis agreed to meet at my flat later that evening.

Lewis ambled into the living room, he flicked his fingers through his blonde back combed hair. He wore a light denim shirt unbuttoned at the collar and a darker pair of Paul Smith jeans. On his feet he had a pair of ubiquitous calf CAT industrial quality boots.

"Is this about what we were talking about the other night?" He asked.

"You're on the ball" I replied, "This is about having fun, guaranteeing your own supply and buying that boat you've been going on about."

"Oh, it's that simple is it?" Lewis said sounding quite dismissive.

"You're the expert, have a scan through this, it's not as simple as poaching an egg but its certainly not rocket fuel science." I passed him my pile of books, Phikal, The Secrets of Metampethamine Manufacture and E is for Ecstasy.

"I'll put some coffee on while you have a look, I've flagged the relevant pages as I see them."
James came through to the kitchen with me and sat himself on the bare iron work surface. I'd decided against chairs in the kitchen, lack of space, lack of light and they'd clutter up the minimalist design.

"What do you think we'll have to do to make this stuff?" asked James.

"I don't really know, well I've read the books and I know what has to be turned into what and so on but really I've no idea how long it'll all take, what the processes actually entail and what the chances of success are."

"Well I suppose it'll be a laugh" he said launching himself off the work surface and over to the fridge where he helped himself to a can of coke. "It's not as if we're proper drugs manufacturers are we? I wouldn't know one end of a Bunsen burner from the other."

I smiled and got Lewis' coffee from the Gaggia machine which was spluttering and gurgling. "It won't be as easy as this," I gestured in the direction of the stainless steel coffee machine.

We'd only left Lewis for about ten minutes but he'd already made his mind up about the job. He knew what we needed and had an idea where it was all coming from. He precised the plan stating that whilst the recipe in Phikal was by far the best in terms of how it was presented for use, that the recipes in the secrets of Metampthamine Manufacture were the more practical because they used fewer hard to get materials. The book it seemed had been written to help people circumvent the swingeing U.S. laws that restricted the production of drugs in clandestine laboratories. English Oil International would be our primary source of materials. Lewis volunteered, I didn't even have to ask him. Some of the items were proscribed and others weren't within the remit of English Oil Internationals business and we didn't want to draw attention to our scheme by ordering them through the company. As for the proscribed items Lewis was fairly confident that he could synthesise them. It would add to the time taken but at least if we were successful we'd be guaranteed pure raw materials. He compared this with the hassle of refining down the essential basis of some commercially available substances which if weren't 100% pure could completely ruin the finished product rendering it useless. A lot of them had added binding or colouring agents. Some of them actually had substances added to make sure that they weren't used for illicit purposes.

"I've tried making my own lysergic acid before, I told you the other night didn't I? said Lewis, I couldn't remember this but recalled Graham saying something along similar lines. "Well I didn't quite get there it's really sensitive stuff, problems with heat and light and all of that but at least the disco burger formula looks a little less volatile. The glassware is no problem I've got my own at work. I never really use it but we couldn't do all of this in there. This is, at the inside a three day job, and that's working round the clock in shifts. I couldn't risk doing this at work and someone walking in and putting two and two together. It's rare enough for me to get my hands dirty in the lab these days but I wouldn't be able to explain what I was doing down there all weekend with a couple of non company employees. What we need is somewhere large well aired, private and where our presence won't raise anyone's suspicions."

I could see what he was driving at. "Like here you mean?" I asked with mock incredulity.

"Yeah, seriously, like here. It's perfect you've got a lot of space a powerful extractor fan in the kitchen, hardly any neighbours to speak of, most of them really live in the country don't they? This is just a block of City pied a teres for all intents and purposes. Its nearly empty at the weekends. You've also got a pretty miserable looking kitchen which we can cheer up no end if this stuff blows up." Said Lewis with an enthusiastic, charismatic logic.

Train of Thought

"What, there's no chance of that is there?" I asked concerned for my kitchen but already completely convinced by Lewis' command of the situation.

"Well you've read these books as well haven't you. We should be all right if we're careful."

James broke his silence, "Has anyone given any thought as to who's going to sell all of this stuff, who's going to bang it up in to pills. I mean to say I can't see us standing in the toilets in The Ministry or the Final Frontier repeating the mantra, saying 'pills' to every Tom, Dick and Harry and pretending to be their own personal apothacory. Even if we managed to smuggle the pills in the first place and that's a risk in itself, it wouldn't be five minutes before the bouncers handed us over lock stock and barrel to the local constabulary, either that or we do it somewhere totally disreputable and the bouncers tax the pills and the cash and give us a good kicking into the process because organising the pills is all part of their job and they don't like competition. The other thing is pills need binding, pressing and stamping, it's a specialist thing. The only alternative is to do them like rhubarb and custards, which are like you know, capsules half red and half yellow. Even that's time consuming and for a lot of punters they don't have the same feel of legitimacy as a regular pill and if you haven't got customer confidence then these things could take forever to sell."

He had a point.

Lewis suggested that James explore these problems and report back in a few days, stressing that no one else was to get even the faintest idea of what was going on. he also said that the process that we'd be using would only make about 4oz of the drug. That would work out at about 100mg per tablet, two hundred and eighty tablets to the ounce, that's 1,040 tablets or 1,000 in round numbers. We'd get £10 maximum if we sold them to a dealer, probably nearer £7 or £8 or £7,000 or £8,000 depending on which way we looked at it.

James quipped that it would be a lot less if we started using them ourselves, suggesting that three hundred and thirty three pills each wouldn't take too long to drop if we tried hard enough.

"No all samples have to be paid for." I retorted, "We have to run a smooth ship here. We're all staying straight when we do this, no ones going to be telling me that they've just fallen in love with the glassware or that the Bunsen burners got the prettiest flame they've ever seen. I want rational focused minds. We can have all the fun we want to have after this is all finished."

" We're not going to make a fortune are we?" said James.

"Well, not with one batch after we've split it between three. That's three into say, £7,500 about two and a half grand each. but what you've got to realise is that once we get it up and running we can up the size of the batch, we could even run parallel operations. No, the first run won't make you rich but the knowledge and expertise will prove invaluable as we progress our secondary careers" said Lewis.

"Once every three weeks, is about right," he continued, "not every three weeks it's best not to stick to patterns in this type of thing, you know what the rest of the group are like they're bound to come up with some ridiculous interpretation as to why the three of us keep dropping out of circulation at the same time. We'll have to be careful as to how we deny what we were talking about in the pub the other night, there are ways of denying things. Personally I'd laugh and go along with it if any of them suggest that I'm performing alchemy with a couple of bottles of essential oil."

"Does it smell at all? asked James I mean to say I don't mind dancing in a club looking like a total E Boat because nobody knows me but if we're cooking this stuff all weekend I don't want the chip shop effect and not be able to get rid of the smell?"

"You'd probably be grateful for it," I quipped, "it'll attract all of those seventeen year old girls that go clubbing in their droves. You could market it, eh? 'Ecstasy the great smell for men!'"

"Hah, Hah." said James rather unimpressed by my attempt at humour.

"Seriously it will smell," said Lewis, "but not obviously, it's rather like a licourice smell. If it tasted like it smelt it would probably taste like root beer but as you know its got an incredibly bitter taste. I suppose you could say that it smells like smoked cocaine."

"I thought that you sniffed cocaine." I said. I'd never had cocaine, never mind smoked it as far as I knew it was taken through the nose.

"Well not that many people smoke it but its just as effective as sniffing it and it means that if you're at a club you don't have to go to the toilets every five minutes. It's a rather non descript industrial smell not too unpleasant but nothing that you'd chose to scent the room with.

Train of Thought

There's no real problem with people getting to know about it on the outside it's not as if its a recognisable a smell as somebody smoking a joint or a whole pile of joint's for that matter. Anyway you've got no neighbours to talk of have you? We'd only start to have problems if we used "the bomb" method of turning phenylacetone into methamphetamine and it er, goes wrong, or full stop if we use it and there's a friendly police linked satellite taking pictures of the area. its not unheard of is it? Since the IRA explosions,the security around here has been awesome, the satellite would pick up the heat of our reaction when we pipe in the hydrogen gas to react with phenylacetone and methyamine. Its almost like an H bomb." explained Lewis.

"E bomb, you mean," said James, " you're not getting me anywhere near that."

"No don't worry we won't actually be using that method but just for the record the reaction is done at a pressure of three atmospheres, that's only thirty pounds per square inch greater than air pressure so there's no chance of wiping out from here to Essex."

"Pity, could have been a bit of fun, not that we'd have had time to laugh." I joked.

"All right, enough of the banter if this isn't going to occupy us for the next seven to ten years then we'll have to keep it to ourselves and that means no one else knowing. No one else." Lewis reiterated at least he had the same ideas as me when it came to security. This is going to be like going to work, there are rules and we're going to be as professional as we are during the daytime. This is going to happen soon, it'll have to be at the weekend, we'll start on Friday lunchtime and hopefully be finished by Monday   midday. It's going to mean a weekend of no clubbing "

James agreed to look into the dealing and pill pressing side of things. We'd have to find out who wanted to buy our product and who could and would pay for it, there was no point making the stuff and having it taken off us at gun point or worse.

Lewis said that we'd have to be careful when the inevitable questions came from the boys as to where we'd been for the weekend and what we'd been up to. Two of us wouldn't be at home, the third would and he'd have his answer 'phone on. All three of us would have our mobiles off all weekend. Quite simply we'd all be away on business if anyone asked, well that was the truth wasn't it in a round about sort of way.

We cracked open a couple of bottles of beer I'd brought back from a trip to France. The boys stayed for quite a while throwing around ideas and discussing what we were going to do at the weekend. I thought about little else for the rest of the evening. There didn't seem to be too much chance of getting caught making these little beauties. The scary bit would be trying to get rid of them. It was no real secret that various clubs and areas of London were supplied by certain gangs and crime families, they'd supplemented their traditional protection money with the profits from the sale of E. We weren't big enough to cause them very much trouble in the way of lost income but from what I'd gathered they didn't like problems of any type. We'd have to try to find out where, if anywhere these people didn't operate. I wasn't too happy about dealing with the gangs after all we had what they wanted, but they were in the position to control the price, because if they ran out of the real thing they'd still be able to sell on duds and cut pills to their regular outlets who wouldn't be in a position to say no. I contented myself with the thought that if it all went well that every three weeks I'd be two and a half grand better off. That was forty to forty five thousand pounds or more tax free, each and every year if Lewis was right.

Degrees of Passion

It had been booked for ages. A cheap weekend in
Amsterdam. Not that type of cheap weekend in
Amsterdam. It was James, Greg, myself a sixty pound
airfare and the first cheap hotel we came across. I'd never
been before and what with all of the excitement about our
little manufacturing industry it didn't really grab me. Still
it was supposed to be the drugs capital of Europe and the
centre of Ecstasy production. I'd read something on the
subject and from what I could gather E wasn't legal
anymore but the law wasn't too harshly enforced.

In England there didn't seem to be a coherent approach
to the issue of illegal drugs. There was no recognition
that pills were used by at least half a million people every
week, that was a huge number of people to alienate
through criminalisation. Not enough thought had been
given to realistic drugs education and licensing. People
might die on ecstasy but that wasn't going to be avoided,
it wasn't going to go away, but it could be minimised.
Ecstasy was proving to be a remarkably safe drug. Each
year more people died from allergies to peanuts and no
one was seriously suggesting the criminalisation of
peanuts. The suggestion that the use of drugs like
ecstasy and cannabis led to the use of addictive drugs
didn't hold water, if it did why hadn't we seen the
hundreds of thousands of ecstasy users since the start of
acid house hospitalised or registered as 'hard drug'
addicts. No, ecstasy was safer than tobacco or alcohol,
those drugs killed hundreds of thousands every year but

the government refused to recognise it. It was a case of better the devil you tax, than the devil you think would be a vote loser.

Come Friday James had decided to drop out. Flu, he said but then again all of us had the flu. Colds, flu's and minor infections seemed to becoming a regular weekly occurrence.

So it was going to be just me and Greg. We'd arranged to meet in a large pub at the Spitalfields end of Liverpool Street Station before we got the train to Stansted. I fought my way through the acrid cigarette smoke which shrouded the crowds of Friday early evening drinkers. He wasn't there. Just me I thought, well that would be a bundle of laughs.

Well happily that wasn't going to be the case, Greg had pulled himself out of the pub and was standing by the platform barrier. He was talking to a young girl with dark bobbed hair and black smiling eyes. I introduced myself and enquired hopefully as to whether she was coming in the place of James.

"No course not, but she'd be a lot more fun than James. This is Penny, she used to work for me" sang Greg, despite his flu he'd obviously had a skinful.

"Hey, Hey, Hey, I am looking forward to this. James reckons that he'll see us out there but I doubt it. See you Pen." He stooped and gave her a sloppy kiss on the cheek.

We got onto the first carriage, only to see the familiar figure of James almost completely hidden by a huge oversize black puffer jacket. He was wearing a black woolly ski hat and a pair of wrap around sun glasses. He sat taking occasional sips from a large carton of milk. He didn't say a word, his coughing did that for him.

I sat down next to him, effectively half on top of and I nudged him in the ribs, pleased to see him and hopeful of a response. Nothing.

"At least you came along we were almost going to draft in one of Greg's friends to take your place. Give it a rest tonight and you'll be in a position to go absolutely mental tomorrow." James grimaced at my suggestion. He must have been in a really bad way.

"None of you idiots have got any drugs on you, 'cos if you have its time to get rid of them before we go through customs?" were the only other words he said for the entire journey. No we hadn't, I didn't like dogs at the best of times and the thought of a springer spaniel going for me was enough to but paid to that. Besides I thought these things were bound to be cheaper over there.

Greg amused himself by trying to drink dry the planes supply of beer, complaining that his attempts were thwarted by the fact that the plane started to descend almost as soon as it took off. We'd almost not got on it in the first place as James was insistent that we volunteered to miss the flight, which was overbooked and be put up at the airlines expense with a bit of spending money thrown in. Common sense prevailed as we eventually persuaded him that Amsterdam might be a little more exciting than Stansted.

It had been a mistake not to book a hotel before we got there. We made a pretty sad sight trudging around Amsterdam full of flu and laden with enough bags for a month never mind a weekend. James suggested we got a taxi from the railway station but Greg said there was no point because it was the back streets we wanted and that it was quicker to walk. The first few places we tried were effectively youth hostels with the promise of music all day and night. Well we were going to go clubbing for that. We eventually found something a little more up to the mark. They'd only let one of us check out the room. James demanded to do it on the basis that he was going to spend most of the weekend in the room so it'd better be to his liking.

He came down in the lift with the receptionist with a look of glee in his eyes. The first positive sign of life all weekend.

"Great, it's got a view over a square and there's a splendid vista of this really different church spire. "said James with a hint of achievement.

Pleased to here him in spirits again I couldn't resist saying,"Oh so you're a buff on ecclesiastical architecture now are you?"

Greg and I left him, tucked up in bed with extra blankets, the television remote, a selection of the dance music magazines, throat lozenges, a carton of milk and two litres of bottled water. Greg reminded him to keep drinking fluids, laughing at the time James had found himself in a South American field hospital after a mornings beach volley ball and a couple of cocktails under the midday sun. Poor sod he'd had to stay there on a saline drip for three days while everyone was enjoying themselves. He wasn't amused, he'd been reminded of the story every time he travelled and it was growing a bit thin. Greg and I went out to catch what was left of the

Degrees of Passion

Friday night. We'd ring James at the hotel in a couple of hours to see if he was feeling up to joining us but there wasn't much chance of that.

I felt like a walk to unwind from the journey but Greg suggested that we went into the closest bar. It was pretty obvious to me that it was a gay bar and not the designer type that you found on darling old, Old Compton Street, no this was leathers, moustaches and a distinct S&M image. There was quite a cruisey atmosphere so, despite the banging house and nu-energy pulsating out onto the street we eventually decided that we'd go on elsewhere.

We passed down an alley in the direction of the general flow. The centre had to be where everyone was going. We emerged out onto a wider and brighter street. There was glass door after glass door. Spaced every six or seven feet, they revealed girls of mainly Asian origin. Scantily clad, some were more or less unclothed. They looked drugged up to the eyeballs. I resisted eye contact but could make out the heroin addicted, pin prick pupils. What should have been alluring was positively repulsive, there was no hint of personal chemistry about these girls apart from that which they regularly and unglamoursly injected. Scantily clad, drugged to the hilt, and pretending to be having a good time. What a contrast to the girls at our top clubs, they too were scantily clad, drugged to the eyeballs but the difference was that they were doing something they wanted to do and were having the time of their lives.

Their audience comprised of both sexes, single lonely men, coach parties replete with guides and groups of boisterous mainly English youths already worse for wear on the local beer.

"Here lets have a quick look," said Greg. I'd seen enough already. It was sad and ridiculous. It couldn't be further from being sexually attractive. Perhaps that's why no seemed to be going into the booths. "Come on, lets find that pub, I could do with a drink now," I told Greg.

Greg picked a Bulldog pub. He'd spent quite a lot of time growing up in the Netherlands and was keen to show me around. He'd told me that it was a cross between a normal pub and one of the so called brown cafes which had cannabis as their main stock in trade. Away from the bustle of the bar and the snooker table was a small reception type table manned by a moustached gentleman who handed us a menu. It was full of dope, line after line of dope, nothing but dope.

"Have you got any pills mate? I asked

"No and you will not buy it here it a restricted hard drug you may only buy soft drugs here." He bellowed, visibly angry. He was obviously annoyed that day after day night after night he got these stupid English tourists asking him the same questions over and over again. I thought about telling him that there had been no real research into ecstasy and that it had been classified as class A rather than B or C because of ignorance of its effects and the lack of any official recognition that it had a real medical use. It had been a better safe than sorry approach. Somehow I didn't think he was ready for a philosophical discussion.

"Only asking, weren't we?" Greg chirped and we left the man to sit at his table in peace.

Degrees of Passion

I actually enjoyed my beer. We looked through the pages out of the Time Out guide to Amsterdam I'd brought with me. We decided to drift on to a couple of the clubs mentioned in there. The first was completely empty. It was about four hours before it was supposed to get really going, well we didn't feel like waiting for four hours so we scored a couple of Es from two locals playing table football in a quiet room. I suppose it would have been a chill out room if there had been anything to chill out from. Seven quid fifty each that wasn't bad. The pills were an offish light blue with a jumping dolphin printed on them. I'd never seen pills like this before but I suppose that was one of the pleasures of travel having new things to try, new places to see and new people to meet. The lads suggested that we should try It or Mazzo, neither of which was too far away. We did our pills there and then. I suppose in a way to gauge the reaction of our suppliers, not that we'd be able to do anything about it if we thought they were duds. They said that they were good but that they took time to come up on. Well I certainly wasn't sure about that. It normally took thirty minutes with me, any longer and I was going to get worried. Well the pills were swimming around down our gullets by now, so there was no going back.

"At least we'll be at the next place before they kick in " said Greg.

Famous last words. Famous last bloody words. Within fifteen minutes or so walking down the street I began to feel a familiar tingle in my spine and my head started to extract pleasure from everything around me.

Degrees of Passion

"Oh, Oh I've got that feeling that I've got to be somewhere five minutes ago," I said amazed at the speed I was kicking in at. I needed to be somewhere, not looking for somewhere. It was always best to do your pill somewhere were you wanted to be, with people you wanted to be with and somewhere where you felt fundamentally comfortable. Not lost in the middle of an unfamiliar city.

"This looks promising," said Greg, pointing to a steel door covered in stretched canvas or sacking. We walked in to the mesmerising interior. It was a visual conundrum of bulging walls, atriums and mezzanine floors. The walls were painted in dark post modern reds and offset by a dazzling display of glass and stainless steel that adorned the stair cases. Most reassuring of all was the fact that it seemed to be populated by normal types who wouldn't look out of place at the Final Frontier, not the fashion conscious melts who frequented some of the the commercial garage nights in London's apparently fashionable circles. There was a restaurant upstairs and the atmosphere was more bar than club.

"We could do with a few more places like this back at home," I said, "We've only got places like Riki Tik and the occasional designer gay bar that comes in the same division."

"That's probably because no one who'd appreciate a place like this drinks that much alcohol anymore," replied Greg.

Well I suppose he had a point if the clubs were open to six a.m. and beyond if you wanted then there was no real reason to go out and mob the pub for a couple of hours before dancing your socks off.

We climbed the glass stairs and stood by the balcony taking in the view, the experience of entering a new world was a little sobering and I only really started to feel the full force of the E kicking in as we stood still and relaxed.

Greg was kicking in as well but after standing there and smiling with me for a few minutes he went off and bought a couple of beers. He offered me one, I couldn't, not now all of this was starting to take place. He just shrugged as if to say all the more for me. I don't know how he did it but I wasn't in the mood to compete with him, I was just going to relax and enjoy myself. I felt a sense of calm contentment, I didn't have to move, I stood by the balcony rail as Greg chirped away, I'd occasionally pat him on the back in a reassuring way. He was happy talking and I was happy to stand and listen to the music.

After a while I just felt a buzz that it was time to move on a bit. Putting thoughts into actions took a while but eventually I went for a walk. I wanted to see what was going on elsewhere, my senses were becoming enhanced, I still didn't want to talk to Greg but whatever it was that I wanted to do I wasn't going to do it where I was. I just followed the staircase down and down again. I found myself in the largest toilets in the world. Yes, they had to be the best toilets in the whole world. I spent forever down there looking around and marvelling at the green, bullet proof glass pissoirs and the polished steel toilet doors. They'd even commissioned taps with brass, glass and steel handles. I was impressed. I got myself a drink of water from those incredibly nice taps. I wanted to tell somebody else about my toilets, just in case they didn't realise that they were within walking distance of the best toilets in the world. I dragged myself away and of the main door which was half open. I told the lady sitting there behind a table. She didn't seem to understand me, undeterred I tried asking her if the Ladies were just as nice. Poor soul she seemed to be losing patience. It wasn't what I'd tried to do. I wanted to make her happy, make any one happy for that matter. It wasn't until I told Greg about this later that I realised that I'd broken the golden rule and not paid the lady for the use of the toilets she looked after. Good job I suppose they were such nice toilets that I'd probably have given her a blank cheque or something.

I walked round the ground floor still happy in my surroundings. This place was amazing. There was a room recessed behind the main open bar area. The walls seemed to curl round and allow you in as if though the eye of a needle. Better still there was a wild mix of music pounding out and lots of people largeing away their Saturday morning. Seemingly familiar faces were gurning to the trippier grooves as the scratching sounds from the DJ booth chopped in and out of the beats. There were raised dance areas to elevate the dancers to higher states. Arm pits seemed to be in fashion as the stripped to the waist brigade, lifted their arms to the ceiling and seemed to be having it all night along. I wanted a piece of this, I eased myself on to the dance floor and when The Future Sound of London's, "Papaya New Guinea" came on, well that was it. Yes, I might have only just discovered this

Degrees of Passion

place but it was the best place in the world. Absolutely. No doubt about that what so ever. I even forgot where I was, which was the way in and out of the room and who I was with. That didn't matter because I wasn't going anywhere this was the only place to be.

I suppose that I'd been in there for about two hours before I remembered that the last I'd seen of Greg he was standing by the balcony talking to himself. I dragged myself away from all of the shiny happy people, got my bearings and made haste to see if Greg was all right. I'd wanted to stay dancing but despite the selfishness of the hedonism, this was still all about camaraderie and empathy, I wanted to see my mate.

Well I shouldn't have worried, he was still there as if he'd been araldited to the floor, talking to an absolutely stunning girl. She was tall, possibly Italian with an olive Mediterranean tan and the most beautiful hair which flowed over her shoulders in one inch diameter curls, half way down her back.

Well, I was impressed. Greg nonchalantly introduced us. She smiled and Greg did all of the talking. Me I just remember having this stupid grin on my face. An E grin, exaggerated by Greg's new friend, Summer's charms. Apparently she'd been dumped by her Dutch boyfriend. Dumped? I thought, how could anyone be that stupid?

I plucked up the courage to talk to her, asking her if she'd got anywhere to stay. She had, she was staying with her ex-boyfriend but was going back to London tomorrow, or rather this morning depending on which way you looked at it. She'd only come out to clear her head and wasn't staying for too long.

Degrees of Passion

Slightly diverted from her charms for a moment I told Greg about the toilets and the dance floor. Summer laughed at my enthusiasm. "They're okay, but I wouldn't describe this place as the best place on earth, One of the best bars in Amsterdam but that's about it. Look, why don't you two give me a ring when you get back. We can go out clubbing if you like, have a really large night out." She started writing down, her name, address and telephone number.

With that I didn't need anymore confirmation that this was the best place on earth. Positively. Absolutely. Definitively. I hadn't really imagined her to be a podium princess or non stop party bunny, but she'd be the type of clubbing partner to take me to celestial ecstasy.

We walked her to the door of the bar and hailed her a rare Amsterdam taxi. She wasn't going far but I insisted that she got a taxi. Summer waved us both good-bye and we exchanged kisses on the cheeks. Now that felt good.

Things didn't seem the same after she left, perhaps it was the E coming down, but anyway we decided to find our way to one of the clubs which we'd heard of.

"Well she's the best looking girl that I've seen you with in along time, an absolute uber babe." I congratulated Greg

"Not far wrong there," said Greg, obviously pleased with himself but I could tell that he wasn't really interested, he talked about girls a lot but he didn't spend that much time with them, he preferred the cut and thrust of life in the pub with the boys and the occasional trip to the casinoor the greyhounds. It's not that he didn't like girls it was just that, what with work and everything else he didn't really have anytime for them.

I knew that one of the first things I was going to do when I got back was to give her a ring and I didn't feel too bad about it either.

We wandered about a bit, I'd come down to about a quarter of the intensity I'd felt in the bar. Greg was up for a few high jinks though. I couldn't work out whether he was off his head or not, one minute he was walking normally down the streets, he next he was uncontrollably breaking into raptures and at one stage he climbed the railings of a street side canal and announced that he was going to jump in. He wasn't. If he was going to jump in he would have done it already, if the water was as beautiful and as inviting as he suggested that would have been it, I would have had to have fished him out. I just smiled at this half suggestion and waited for him to join me walking down the street. He did and eventually we found our way to IT. A huge cavernous hanger, rammed with mainly gay men and women. Outrageous dancers of both sexes performed in cages. They were trussed and chained gyrating to the blasting Hi -Energy music. It was more disco based than I'd expected and in a way it reminded me a bit of Heaven in London. Heaven had a great house night on Fridays called Garage which pushed hard Nu energy in the main room, with New York style garage grooves on a smaller upstairs floor. Saturdays at Heaven were a little like Saturdays at IT from what I could gather with the emphasis on camper, cheesier sounds. Oh well, we were there and we might as well make the most of it.

Degrees of Passion

We tried to score pills. This was Amsterdam in a club with two and a half thousand people and no there were no pills, this had to be retribution for doing something really bad.

I decided to dance anyway. I'd always maintained that it was possible to have a good night out if you were drug free. Well I wasn't drug free just now but I wasn't high either. I gave it loads, somehow finding a second wind from somewhere. I noticed a difference about the place. People didn't make as much eye contact as in the straight clubs I'd been to. I put it down to the fact that this was a bit of a cruisey joint and well if you started to look at someone then it might have initiated the wrong, or right for that matter, response depending on which way you looked at it. I am not saying that it was as stand offish as an old style discotheque but there was just that slight perceptible difference. It might have also had something to do with all the bottles of beer which were being drunk.

I felt a little tired after half an hour and went back to see what Greg was up to. He was asleep, slumped over the bar. He nodded in recognition as I nudged him.

I laughed as he recalled, "they tried to throw me out, said that I couldn't sleep here but if I've paid to get in surely I can do what I like in here as long as I'm nice to people. I mean to say me sleepings hardly going to raise eyebrows in a place like this. Did you see those blokes on stage before? It's anatomically impossible, size of them absolutely disgusting, I've heard of silicone implants, what do these geezers implant, elephants trunks or what?"

Degrees of Passion

I told Greg that I'd missed the dancers on the stage but I'd seen them on the bar just by where he was slumped.

"What!" He seemed genuinely taken a back.

"You seemed to be quite relaxed about it all the bloke was nearly tripping over you as he danced round the pole at the end of the bar. You were probably being asked to move out of his way."

"Hum, well whatever, don't get me wrong I've got nothing against places like this but at the end of the day the music isn't up to scratch, there are no drugs to be had and I am getting a little worried about being trodden on by some half naked geezer in rubber and chains strutting around flaying a fire hose."

"Alright I said getting the hint, lets move on its a big city and its still not time for breakfast. We can always give James a ring to see if he fancies joining us and livening up proceedings."

Hotel reception explained that he was probably sleeping and that they normally didn't put calls through at this time of night. We persevered and eventually a feeble voice asked,

"What is it?"

"Fancy going to a club, big boy?" enthused Greg who'd got his energy back.

The line went dead and we drew our own conclusions from that.

"Well suit yourself then," Greg laughed.

We walked down the canal flanked streets, past row after row of shuttered tall dockside buildings. Amsterdam's houses gave the impression that her populace was sleeping but the constant flow of early morning revellers belied the fact. Queues snaked round the corner of several smaller looking clubs. Rather like in London where lots of clubs seem to get a second wave of punters at three or four in the morning. Neither of us felt like queuing after all we'd had quite a full night of revelling and what with the travelling, despite the adrenaline rush of being abroad we were both starting to get understandably tired.

I was flyered for a club which promised Billy Nasty, John Kelly, Jon Pleased Wimmin, "and other top English Club DJs" as future attractions. Well that sounded more like it.

Greg decided that he'd had enough and that he'd walk back and clear his head. I eventually found the club in question. Ominously there wasn't a queue and I was disappointed to find that there was only a few select clubbers in there. They were making the most of the empty dance floor. I could tell that this place would be packed in a few weeks time once a buzz got around about it, the music was good progressive house mixing classics like Leftfield's "Song for Life," with great garage like Alison Limerick's 'Where Love Lives." and a few Patrik Prins tunes. It wasn't busy enough for me to ask around for pills or whatever I just sat and soaked it all in. Strangely enough no one came up to me for a chat and I left before it finished but that was a reflection on me not the club. I had a vague idea of where the hotel was. I followed the canals as the sun cast the first rays of the new day across the sleeping town.

Remarkably about two bridges from home I saw the unmistakable silhouette of Greg standing by the railings.

Degrees of Passion

"Been mugged, should have known, when he asked me for a light, he had a ciggie in his hand at the time as soon as I got my matches out there was a knife to my cheek."

I found the entire concept hard to comprehend. Not that I didn't believe him. No it wasn't that, it was feeling that I got from the E, everyone was okay and that there was no need to do things that way.

"I am all right though I just kept him talking and gave him the line about all my cash being in my pocket and if he wanted it he could have, so like the geezer, he's big and he's black, well he goes through my front pockets saying that if he found that I was lying to him about the amount of cash I had on me or if I had cash anywhere else that he'd cut me. Well all he found was about thirty or forty Guilders in my front pocket. Muggers money you know, I'd shoved the rest of it down my undies, can't be too careful these days. Oh yeah and he missed this as well he said taking out a huge lump of dope. Got this from round the corner. Fancy making in the direction of the Hotel and having a puff with James?"

Well I didn't smoke, so no, I wasn't up for that but he was obviously still a little shook up over what had happened so I slapped on the back and we made our way back to the Hotel. We'd both agreed that, that was enough for one evening.

We both jumped on James bed when we got back. He'd been fast asleep and wasn't particularly pleased to see us.

"First the bells, now you lot," James sounded half asleep, "that bloody church has been chiming every two minutes, this place should have double glazing or something it's been a nightmare trying to get any sleep and what with you two ringing me,"

"Should have come out with us then, we've had a sort of varied night, fancy a pill, a bit of blow or a cup of coffee?" asked Greg

"I know that this is Amsterdam but you've got to be off your bloody rockers if you think that I am going to be skinning up this time in he morning, anyway what have you got?" asked James, "what were the local pills like? Have you got any for me, not for now like, but for later on."

At least James was starting to show a bit of spirit. Greg forgot all about his gear when it became clear that no one else was interested. We all stayed crashed on James's bed and watched children's telly, we'd come all the way to Amsterdam and they had ITV and BBC on the satellite. It wasn't until about midday after a couple of cat naps and a shower that we went off in the search of breakfast. Walking down the narrow streets bustling with Saturday shoppers none of were prepared for the dangers of the trams that appeared with what seemed to be only a moments warning. Then there were the cyclists. They wove an impossible pattern through the milling crowds. Collisions seemed inevitable but we eventually made it to a large McDonalds. We'd all wanted to go somewhere different. I wasn't really hungry, Greg wanted to go to a pub and James wanted to go back to bed. It was an uninspired choice but we'd lost our spirit of adventure for the moment. James went back to hotel, I went off in search of the art galleries and Greg went off in search of a pub that was showing the rugby international.

Degrees of Passion

On my way north out of the centre, close to the main galleries I stumbled on a drugs shop. It wasn't anything like the Bulldog pubs or the so called brown cafes. This was a shop with books on the walls, bongs and other smoking paraphernalia all over it. I asked for pills and got the standard reply. I hadn't upset the shop attendant as much as the last time. He was adamant that he didn't have any and that he didn't have any legal substances that were in the least like E. What he did show me, with a sense of pride was a white paper bag containing two six or seven inch mushrooms which he told me were South American in origin, although I couldn't see first how it could have been economical to import, or practical for that matter because mushrooms deteriorate so quickly, besides there were normally strict rules as to what type of plant and vegetable matter could be imported within the EEC, to do more with the spread of agricultural disease more than anything else.

I'd always thought that magic mushrooms were smaller but he told me that there were lots of different varieties and that the ones he was showing me were some of the best. I wasn't sure, they didn't look too appetising and I wasn't sure as to what could be crawling around inside them. What really persuaded me not to buy them was the fear of having a bad trip on them. No, I was away from home not feeling 100%, whilst I'd heard that you stood less chance of a bad trip on mushrooms than on a blotter of LSD. I'd also heard that a trip depended on your state of mind and mine wasn't quite right at the moment. So I did what Nancy Regan suggested and "just said No to the drugs." What I'm sure she should have said was "Just say Know", that sounded a far better idea.

The rest of the day was spent trawling the Van Gough Museum, thinking about our little plan. I hadn't had the chance to talk to James about it all weekend but perhaps that was for the best Greg was there and he was bound to pick up on something, More to the point Lewis wasn't around and it didn't seem right to make plans without consulting him. Van Gough's profligacy astounded me, I wondered what it would have been like to have all of your work on show to any one who wanted to see it, not just the acclaimed masterpieces but all the Sunday afternoon formative doodlings. I wasn't too sure that he'd be too happy to have moved so rapidly from not having sold anything to having his whole life's work flash in front of anyone who had the stamina to battle their way round this demanding visual feast.

The modern sculpture garden I stumbled on coming back into town was more to my liking, at least I could view that in peace.

Remarkably I bumped into Greg again, more or less in the same place as last night. Fortunately there was no bad news this time. He bubbled with excitement about the group he'd met in the bar whilst watching the rugby. He'd drunk them under the table. Not satisfied with his alcoholic haze he was planning ahead. We didn't have any pills for the evening and wasn't it time that we scored some? Greg suggested trying a street dealer, there were loads of them in the seedier areas. That didn't sound such a good idea, I thought that he should have learned his lesson from the night before about trusting strange men on dark and dangerous streets. Still there was something about his charismatic drunken charm which led me to follow him on such a dubious mission. On the way we tried one of the numerous sex shops which displayed leather, rubber and chains in forms and varieties that stretched even our over active imaginations. We weren't interested in the sad magazines or sex aids, just the poppers. They were twice the price as in Old Compton Street but we bought a couple of bottles anyway.

Greg quipped, "if we wanted to get rid of our colds that these little babies will do it."

I smiled not bothering to say that whilst they may alleviate the problem of blocked sinuses they were guaranteed to give you a stinking head ache.

We moved on and found a long dark street. I couldn't work out as to whether the men hanging around doorways were pimps, pushers or rent boys. Greg seemed to know and he led me to the end of the street where it joined onto a quieter more respectable street.

"Here, this one over here, lets see what he's got." said Greg as he went over to a shortish man, a swarthy South American in his forties. He had a battered leather jacket, more of a blazer than a bomber jacket and a black leather skull cap.

"You want heroin, crack, cocaine, cannabis, ecstasy?" He'd guessed that we were English. That was something, we'd been mistaken for Germans the night before and I wasn't sure whether that was a compliment or not.

"Yeah, we want to have a look at some of you pills,"

"Say what?"

"Ecstasy," I reiterated.

Degrees of Passion

"Oh yes, the ecstasy is very good, you will come this way with me, he turned, beckoning us to follow him into an alley way."

"Oh no," Greg replied, if you want our business come over here and we can do this in privacy on the street corner."

Our man obliged, we stood around him so as not to attract the attention of the occasional homeward bound shopper. "Very good ecstasy," he said, "you try some to see that it tastes all right. Well it had that bitter taste but so did a million and one different types of legally manufactured substances which you could buy over the counter at the local pharmacy back home.

"No this is shite," said Greg,

"No it is good", our man sounded upset.

"How much have you got then?"

"Just these," he said lifting out about fifteen tablets.

Well we'll take them all, said Greg as he snatched them off our man who didn't seem to know what was going on. Neither did I. Greg pulled me away and we sprinted down the street away from the bellowing dealer. Greg didn't seem too worse for wear from the afternoons drinking, it was probably that which had spurred on the bravado and guile needed to pull off such a coupe. That and the pride which had been dented by last nights mugging. We lost our man quite easily, he was probably just as surprised as I was at the tables being turned like that. When we'd finally stopped running I shouted at Greg, "Dickhead, you bloody dickhead," feeling the adrenaline bring a smile to my face. Like a pair of mischievous children we congratulated each other and told and retold the story to each other on the way back to see James. We couldn't wait to tell him of our exploits.

That night we went out to the Mazzo club where we should have gone the night before. We had a wild trouble free night. All three of us were flying, the only thing which took my mind off the night in hand was a nagging feeling that I should have spent so much more time with Summer than I did last night. Who knows I might not see her again and I'd only have myself to blame. It was one of those persistent thoughts which sometime grow out of proportion when you're high on E. I was sure though that I wasn't blowing this out of proportion I really did like her and I was desperate to see her when I got back to London. She was the best thing to happen to me since I'd fallen in love with the E. I hadn't felt like this for a long time, I told myself not to be stupid, she probably hadn't got over her last boyfriend, she probably wouldn't like me but I had this overriding hope that the smile and kiss she'd given me last night showed that she felt the same way as I did. Or did it, she'd kissed Greg as well but I didn't remember her smiling at him like that. I worked it round and round in my brain and the message from Uncle E was that it was all right. I hoped so.

Coming back we got stopped at the airport of course for drug running. I was asked whether I'd been offered anything by anyone. My reply was half truth and half fiction, yes we had been offered drugs but no we hadn't bought any. Well I suppose that it was almost true in the case of Greg, he'd been offered some and no he hadn't bought any, he'd only bloody well stolen them! I cannot remember whether he still had any on him when we were stopped but knowing Greg that was unlikely, he treated life as a bit of a challenge and the concept of saving something for later was alien to him. We weren't searched and we made our separate weary ways home.

Strings of Life

Strings of Life

It was the early hours of the evening before I got back to the Barbican. I wanted to go straight to bed. I still had a job and I planned to keep it that way but I knew that if I left everything until the morning that I was bound to be late. I turned up the Hi Fi in my bedroom and the sounds of the Deep Dish and Yoshitoshi mix of Submarine by Submarine floated through into the lounge. I put a pair of jeans in the freezer, I'd heard that it was easier to get the chewing gum off them when they were frozen. I kept on finding the stuff stuck absolutely everywhere. The need to chew to stop jaws grinding coupled with the lack of chairs in clubs meant that sitting on a piece of discarded gum was an inevitable, weekly experience.

I ironed a shirt for the next day as I shuffled through my mail. I'd also rewound the video and was watching this weekends episode of BPM, the only TV programme to acknowledge the existence of dance music. It came from the swish, happy and glamorous Swoon in Stafford. Swoon looked great lots of ultimate party people largeing up their weekend. I made a mental note to go sometime. I'd also checked my E-mail and flicked back through the messages on the answer machine, most of them about going out here or there. It was only as I was going back through to the bedroom that I heard a voice that I didn't recognise. Female and interesting. I went through and turned it back. There was no mistaking who it was this time.

81

Strings of Life

"Hi, Jerry, it was Jerry wasn't it? I can't remember whether Greg said that you preferred Jerry or Jeremy. Well it's me, Summer, from Amsterdam, you've probably gathered that I hate answer machines but I thought I'd leave you a quick message to see whether you could give me a ring at work tomorrow, well when I say tomorrow I mean Monday if you see what I mean, bye, speak soon."

Well that had put a different complexion on things. Good news, to put it mildly. I went to bed knowing that tomorrow wasn't going to be that bad after all.

I managed to get to work for six and work through until about ten thirty. It was only then that I began to crash, the extra energy I'd got from Summers call started to rapidly recede when I actually thought about calling her. I don't know what it was, it wasn't as if she would wonder why I was calling, after all it was her who'd asked me to ring her. I just couldn't lift the phone I just sat there with my feet on the table with a million thoughts rushing through my mind. Post E anxiety had struck again.

"Bloody state of you," Middlehurst, my manager bellowed, waking me up as he marched into my office. You're no use to me like that I've been on a stag weekend and I am sure that I don't look half as bad as you, just pull yourself together, wake up and get some work done, you'll be wanting me to put a good word into Hyde about you next time your appraisal comes up."

"I'm okay," I said aware of my faltering voice, "just feeling a bit queasy, probably the dregs of that flu from last week." He seemed happy enough and I put the raised voice down to the hangover that he was probably still nursing. I'd have to be more careful in the future though.

Strings of Life

Hyde was our senior partner, an enigmatic, quiet but likeable, unassuming bloke who it didn't pay to get on the wrong side of. He'd certainly have something to say if he thought that I wasn't up to being a partner. I was fairly certain that Middlehurst wouldn't say anything but next time I played Hyde at squash I'd try to get on his right side by carefully letting him beat me. E might be the language and food of the clubs but it was still a controlled drug and frowned upon in the circles that I mixed in at work.

I tried Summer again at midday, just my luck she was out at lunch. I had more luck with Lewis and James. The latter was having the same problems as me but we all agreed that we'd meet at my flat later that evening to discuss drug production.

I got hold of Summer at the sixth or seventh time of asking. I'd lost the earlier inhibitions and we talked like long lost friends. She suggested that we had a drink after work. Dam, I couldn't I was already meeting the boys and that was a serious engagement. That was business and I'd already got into enough grief today for mixing the two. No, it would have to be tomorrow. Well of course she couldn't make that so we settled for lunch on Tuesday. That seemed the best course of action. We might have been getting on like a house on fire on the 'phone but I had only just met her and a lunch date could end conveniently non committal if things looked if they weren't going to work out.

That evening Lewis arrived late but in good spirits.

"Whatcha boys, I've got a few things sorted at work, I've got," he said, prompting himself from a list, "A thermometer, a still head with a thermometer holder, a vacuum water pump, electric vacuum motor, a vacuum adapter, a couple of condensers, a separatory funnel, a claissen adapter, loads of round bottomed flasks, 3000ml, 1000ml, 2000ml, 500ml and 250ml, loads of plain glass tubing, loads of Erlenmeyer flasks, a Buchner filtering funnel for the filtering flask, a single burner element buffet range with infinite temperature control, ring stands and clamps to hold all of this beautiful glass wear together. Most of it was just around in my lab and available the rest will be with me by tomorrow. It's staying at work until the last minute but I need to move some of the chemicals that I've got. I don't want some bright spark of a trainee deciding that he knows exactly what all these cookie chemicals are for and telling anyone. Jerry, you'll have to help me out. I'm not suggesting that you keep them all here but you'll need to get a locker at Liverpool Street Station, change it every twenty four hours mind you. We'll have them all in a sports bag. The other thing is these books, lose them somewhere for a while, chuck them if you have to but we don't want them around, they'd be useful evidence if anyone tried to put a conspiracy charge on us."

I agreed, after all it would be safer than having all of the equipment in my flat for longer than was absolutely necessary.

"There's one problem," said Lewis

"And just what is that? " asked James.

"Well we need a starting point for the process, like safrole which is the main constituent of sassafras oil. That comes from a shrub which is widely available in North

America, but impossible to find over here. I don't think that it's illegal. I know that isosafrole is illegal but that doesn't mean that the oil its self is proscribed but anyway we've got to find some of this stuff otherwise we'll never get off the blocks." Said Lewis with a degree of concern.

"Well how are we going to do that, James and I have got no access to things like that? What about getting it direct from North America." I said

"Well there's the time problem with that we're supposed to be starting pretty soon aren't we?" replied Lewis.
"There'd be nothing to stop us flying over is there? Its only six or seven, hours isn't it?" asked James

"Or more realistically get some one to ship the stuff across. Anyone know anyone in North America." I said.

"Ritchie Hawtin, Jeff Mills, Derek May and Juan Atkins," quipped James, naming some of his favourite DJs.

"No this is serious," replied Lewis, "and rather than being a question of who we know over there it's who we can trust and that's causing me a few problems because we don't want anyone else to even suspect what we're up to and I think that an order for a couple of pounds of sassasfras oil mind put a few minds in motion."

"I don't mind flying over for it," said James, "really it would be no problem I could get the time off work."

Lewis stretched full length on the black leather and chrome Le Corbisheir chaise longue, extending his arms behind him he stared intensely at the ceiling. He resonated an infectious air of relaxation. If he was tense about all of this he wasn't going to let us know. I reminded myself that this was about concentration, playing for ninety minutes and not taking your eye off the ball.

Lewis said that if he couldn't think of a solution by the morning then James would be flying to Toronto tomorrow afternoon. He knew someone out there who wouldn't ask too many questions, he'd be our last resort. hopefully we'd be able to get what we needed over the counter.

James looked a little stunned at all of this, I don't think that he'd really expected Lewis to ask him to go.

"Either you're in or you're out." demanded Lewis paternalistically.

"I know but .....Yes okay" James convinced himself.

"Good lad," Lewis got up off the chaise longue and gave him a hug.

We drew matters to a close not long after that. I arranged to meet Lewis early the next morning. His parting shot was that I should buy several rolls of black plastic bags and a supply of masking tape. "For the kitchen laboratory area, don't want to leave any tell tale signs do we."

Ecstasy was all over the news the next day. Some poor girl was in a coma, the latest ecstasy related victim to be championed by the media. Moral indignation was inflamed as her caring loving parents vented their grief on the 'bastard pushers' who they wanted to see strung up.

There was no acknowledgement that the nature of the beast was such that teenagers like their daughter probably regarded E much as they had regarded alcohol when they were teenagers. It might not be 100% safe but neither was alcohol or tobacco and there was no cry for these to be criminalised. It was the very beer swilling, hard drinking, quarter bottle of scotch a day Fleet Street hack who'd die of alcohol related heart or liver disease within the next five or ten years that was fuelling the fire.

Ecstasy might not have had the benefits of the rigorous pharmaceutical testing that most drugs had to adhere to but then again it wasn't being used for the same reasons that prescription drugs were normally used . It was a recreation drug. Of course it was unfortunate that it wasn't being used for the marriage guidance, anti depression and pain alleviation purposes suggested by Alexander Shulgin. That couldn't be contemplated until attitudes progressed and there was a sea change in political opinion as to the legal position of drugs in society.

Even the Labour party was forbidding its members to talk about drugs. With this degree of moral repulsion by our elders there was no way that the voice of a generation was going to be heard. More importantly the real issue would be ignored. Valuable time which could have been used to try to make what we do safer was lost in the ranting and raging of a press that didn't know or care what was going on. There were no headlines asking for more free water, more chill out areas at clubs and better common sense education on the issue. Only magazines like Mixmag bothered to consider the real issues. No newspaper or anti drugs campaign, was going to win over the hearts and minds of a generation if it told you to imagine taking ecstasy as being like trapped in a house, fully clothed under the duvet, with the heating fully turned on. Not when most young people knew that

what it was really like was all about enjoying yourself.
Having the time of your life. There are far more lottery
winners each week than ecstasy related deaths.

There was hysteria that tablets might be adulterated
with something other than pure ecstasy. Of course they
would be. A dose of E is effective at about 100-130mg
even with a tablet the size of an aspirin there is going to
be something in there more than the actual MDMA.
Probably lactose or another benign substance to bind the
active chemical. It was becoming increasingly clear that
there was no such thing as a normal dose because there
was no such thing as a standard tablet. There was
however no hard evidence that rat poison or other
dangerous substances were being put into the drugs. If
there were major variants in the tablets then these
normally meant that the dose was less effective, for
example, stimulants like ephedrine, ketamine, ventloin,
caffeine and other members of the MDA family of
amphetamines were being used to cheat clubbers of what
they'd supposedly paid for. This was an unregulated
business. There were no factory shops to dispose of
substandard goods at a reasonable price and no effective
controls to ensure that you got what you paid for and
effectively knew what you were taking.

Holland had schemes where tablets could be tested in
clubs. This meant that the trade in rogue pills had almost
stopped over there. Some suggested that this was the
reason for all of the impure or dud pills that were
available in our clubs. Well it might have contributed to it
but I suspected that it had more to do with the greed of
domestic suppliers eager to eke the largest available

profit from the trade. Surely the government had to do something about it. Half a million pills a week at fifteen quid a time was an awful amount of money. It must be affecting the revenues of the breweries, who are still smarting after the opening up of the cross channel duty restrictions. Any business that was worth seven and a half million a week had to be brought within the remit of the established economy. It was almost four hundred million a year. It was almost as big an earner than the national lottery. Perhaps when that particular penny dropped the exchequer might exercise some common sense.

Until then we'd just have to assume that no one had bothered to evaluate all of the facts and if they had, then they were too scared to do anything about it. Our benevolent government had got it's priorities mixed up, too bothered to be seen to be wholesome and caring than addressing the real problem.. It was too damm interested in votes, rather helping to improve the quality of existence for those who had made certain decisions as to how they wanted to live their lives.

I met Lewis near Liverpool Street. James wouldn't have to go to Toronto after all we'd be able to use calamus instead. It would take longer but it would save the hassle of going transatlantic. James had been relieved to say the least. I left Lewis, deposited my bag in the lockers as planned, now at least I could get to work and concentrate on meeting Summer at lunch time.

I had that Tuesday feeling, full of anxiety and depression and while one minute I perked up with the thought of meeting Summer, the next I was down being swamped by a tidal wave of despair and depression, brought on by too many Es, all of the travelling and a distinct lack of sleep and food. She didn't want to see me, I wasn't looking at my best, perhaps it was Greg she thought she was meeting. Then just when I'd decided that it was all futile, self confidence returned with a vengeance.

A Higher State of Consciousness

Lunch went well with Summer. She was every inch as beautiful I'd remembered, which was quite something, I'd been off my head in Holland. I don't really think that she knew that. If she did she didn't mention it. We sat and chatted for a while. Her large animated dark eyes and smiling lips were occasionally hidden by the coils of healthy black curly hair which flowed down her back. She didn't have time to eat lunch but we agree to meet again in the evening. I suggested dinner, somewhere special perhaps. We settled for one of the smart new restaurants off Old Compton Street. Of course I was late. I never used to be late for anything, it was a knock on effect of the E. If she was annoyed she certainly didn't show it. She made me feel relaxed. I just had to sit back and do the listening. She did all the talking, she talked for ages about nothing in particular but that didn't matter, I just enjoyed the sound of her voice. Her verve picked me up, happily I had an appetite and I'd finished before she'd seemed to have started her food. It wasn't my bad table manners, just that she was spending too much time talking to be able to eat. She rattled off stories with the speed of a racing commentator. She told me that she hadn't been to any of the clubs I knew but had mentioned them in Amsterdam to try to impress me. What did impress me was that she was being honest with me. I got the picture that she was a level headed girl who hid behind an extremely lively exterior. Nothing wrong with that I thought I wasn't in the market for someone who

91

wanted to live life twice the speed I was doing at the moment. She had the right type of balance and I felt reassuringly at home with her after such a short time

She let me finish off her food and wasn't afraid to joke that I was looking a bit peaky, she was right, it was the effects of my 'E-Plan' diet. I didn't take it the wrong way, realising that it was just a manifestation of her ability to say things as they were without causing offence. We went round the corner to the Riki Tik bar which was full to burst so we ended up in the Freedom Cafe. I liked the happy, cool ambience, modern interior and the hard, well mixed music but we didn't stay too long as I could see that she wasn't sure what to make of the place and its predominantly gay clientele. I also noticed that our body language was attracting a few disapproving glances. Fair enough I thought, If when in Rome you upset the Romans its probably best to move on.

It was getting late and Summer was getting worried about work. She had to go home and finish something off. I cannot remember what it was that changed her mind but eventually we decided to get a taxi back to the Barbican.

It took forever to hail a taxi and when we did we sat in traffic for ages. If I'd known her better I'd have suggested getting out and walking for a bit, anything to escape the perpetual Soho gridlock. I was afraid that she'd get bored or change her mind and get a tube home. She'd stopped talking and I saw that as a bad sign. She was probably as anxious about all of this as me. When we left the West End I finally relaxed leant back into the seat, put my arm round her and it felt okay again. We did a detour to

A Higher State of Consciousness

Brick Lane to pick up some bagels. She'd never been to the 24 hour Bagel Bake before. I grinned as I handed her a salt beef and mustard bagel, saying "try this you weren't eating earlier."

" Do you normally cut out the flash meal and just bring your girlfriends here?" She joked, happily eating the suberb food in the somewhat incongrous surroundings.

We held hands as we walked along the well trodden Barbican walkways. "The yellow brick road," she said, laughing at the yellow line painted on the pavement to direct visitors. The complex seemed deserted, there were no other pedestrians and only about ten percent of the flats were visibly lit.

I'd planned to give her a tour of the flat but the coffee machine came first. I turned on the Gaggia, she seemed impressed as I banged out the old filter trays. As I turned past her I stopped, held her and we kissed. I forgot the coffee and we made our way to my bed room. Fully clothed she jumped on to my bed and under the duvet. "you're very naughty, you know," she said as she pulled me on to of her. At least I wasn't on one tonight, I'd heard conflicting stories of how it affected you. Greg told me it gave him a "cock of steel", his words not mine and that it was impossible to come on the stuff. James had complained that he could barely get an erection on E but that Claire had told him that this was more the effect of pure speed. James being James joked about E giving him overdue E-jeculation, whatever that was

The next morning we lay there with the curtains fully open basking in the brilliant sunshine and taking in the view across the city. I wondered what it would have been like to have dropped an E together, not for any sexual kick but just so that we could explore each other. Well we didn't need it we were doing a pretty good job of getting to know each other and for all I knew she wasn't in the slight bit interested in drugs of any description, I'd started to assume that lots of people that I met did drop pills but I was careful not to mention it in conversation until I was convinced of it.

I got up and turned on the hi-fi. Music had been a constant companion since I'd been introduced to Uncle E. My record collection grew almost with the day. What was it going to be? Hard house, techno, ambient? I'd play safe with the Graeme Park side of the Cream live CD. It was good garage and quite a bit of it had charted at one time or another. Rightly or wrongly on the scene it was known as the type of music that girls liked. Coincidentally I'd been looking through the A-Z one day and saw that there's an area called Graeme Park near the bottom of the M1 and wondered if this was all part of a DJ attempt at world domination?

I was late already and Summer agreed to leave after me so that I could get to the office on time. I left her a spare set of keys which she'd post through the letter box.
It was only when I'd left that I realised that I'd left all of my pills in the fridge, in what I knew to be the empty milk carton. If she used that surely she'd look inside and find half a dozen or so pills. That wouldn't do, if she was going to find out about all of this it would be direct from me.

I nearly asked the taxi driver to stop, but if I went back I'd be late again and she'd wonder why I'd come back

A Higher State of Consciousness

after fifteen minutes just to get a carton of milk. It wasn't as if we were bereft of corner shops in the City.

I just had to get on with it. I'd ring her at lunch time and I'd be able to tell if anything was wrong. I rung home at eleven o'clock. It was just the answer machine. That was good news I'd half expected battalions of drug squad officers answering the phone, asking how many pills I wanted and how long this Jerry bloke had been supplying me for.

Thankfully I was wrong on both counts, when I rang her she mentioned, without prompting that she'd had to dash for work as soon as I left and had settled for brunch in the in-house cafe. It had taught me a lesson though. From now on there was no way that I was keeping anything incriminating in the flat, at all . Especially with the plans to make the stuff. I needed a safety deposit box. Two of the establishments had been on TV recently due to robberies. Lightening wouldn't strike twice. There'd been a change of management, the old team were currently on a long holiday at Her Majesties Pleasure.

I went mid afternoon, taking a late lunch so as to miss any rush. It was like a film, everyone called me sir and I was given privacy as I put my measly haul into the box. I had twenty four access, a digital locking system, which was number rather than key based. The beauty of it all was that even if something happened there was nothing to link me with this place.

Work was going fine I had two new diversions in my life but they were positively refreshing and causing me no problems. Today if anything they helped fill a gap in the diary, it was Wimbledon again as usual I had four tickets to entertain one of our more valued clients, they'd dropped out at the last minute so I'd been given clearance to use the tickets as I wished. Summer could make it, so could James and to make up the numbers I asked Summer to bring one of her friends. I'd half expected a woman but Summer brought along a friend from Amsterdam who was working in London. Dick was involved in finance but I could tell that he wasn't as straight as the average city financier. During a break in the play I sent James and Summer to get some food and arranged to meet them on the grass in the middle of Aorangi Park. Dick and I skirted round the topic of clubbing, mentioning selective bits from my recent trip to Amsterdam. I was effectively waiting for him to take the bait. It was one of those conversations where you're not sure what's the right thing to say.

Dick being Dutch laughed and said, "You English you're always so polite about everything, what you really want to ask me about is drugs in Amsterdam, don't you?" I was slightly taken aback but relieved at his comments, here I was on Company time talking about drugs to a total stranger. "Yes." was all I said. He went on to tell me that he was able to get anything he wanted back home and that there was no worries about purity or law enforcement. He was shocked at the prices in London but hadn't brought anything with him. He could put me in touch with someone back home if I wanted to risk bringing anything over here. I was gobsmacked at his straightforward approach to all of this. I wasn't in need of anything just now and not for a long time if our plans went to the book but I took his number anyway, he'd be fun to have on the clubbing scene.

James and Summer came back. and Dick said to them looking at me and smiling "I've just been telling Jerry about risks, what was it Jerry? Why did the Actuary cross the road?"
"I've absolutely no idea, why did the Actuary cross the road?" replied James who'd obviously been on the Champagne.

"Because he did it last year."

Part of the next afternoon was spent at my dentists. I'd been reminded to go on two counts, firstly I was getting worried that all of the teeth grinding business might have been doing some damage, a friend said that she knew someone who'd had teeth just drop out when they were on E. The second reminder to go was courtesy of the TV. There was a fly on the wall surveillance programme about Scotland Yards anti robbery squad. I sat transfixed recognising the bank in question and when the officers made their hit I realised that the staircase they were thundering down was my dentists, the distinctive peel of the reception bell being triggered as they ran out in the street to pounce on their prey.

The robbers were caught in spectacular style. Me? Well, thankfully at least my teeth were still intact.

I saw quite a lot of Summer over the next few days, I was starting to include her in alot of my plans but that hadn't introduced her to E yet so when the boys mentioned the idea of going to Ibiza for a long weekend that counted her out, that and the fact that it was a boys thing.

A Higher State of Consciousness

I think it was James' idea we'd fly over from Thursday to Monday so that we didn't have to miss too much time at work and that we wouldn't have to interrupt any of the weekend with travelling. There were going to be quite a few of us, Lewis, James, Jeff and Greg but when it came to finalising the plans we met in the Piano and Pitcher in Dean Street and only Jeff, James and myself turned up. The rest had various excuses most of them work related.

We stood around a table examining the Kiss FM guide to Ibiza which had come out of one of the Clubbers Guide flyer packs which had been left on my windscreen after a long nights clubbing somewhere. The guide was about the size of the table and as we unravelled it we caught the attention of a couple of lads, dressed as if they'd come straight from the office and as I started to explain to Jeff and James where was best to stay and which clubs were the ones to go to we were interrupted by the lads who told us that they'd been over to Ibiza in 1989

They described it as the best place in the world and that they'd literally had the time of their lives there. They weren't going back this year or any year for that matter, it had been so good that there was no way that if they went back it could live up to their expectations. They were informative rather than bragging as they told us all about the clubs out there and their experience of the best clubs from 1989. They mentioned Rage and Shoom, two of the original London rave clubs with absolute reverence and said that they didn't think that anything would be ever be able to compare with them. James had a point though when he said that whilst he didn't doubt what they said that this scene was all about enjoying yourself and there was nothing from stopping the Eurobeat 2000 night next door at Gossips being the best night ever if you wanted it to be the best night ever, clubbing was all about putting something in to it not just expecting to have a good time.

James and Jeff had already booked the time off work and I thought that it would be a formality. Well that's what I thought. The next day I was told that I had meetings on the days in question and there was no way that I could get out of them. That was the end of my holiday plans. I sat in my office unable to concentrate when I vaguely became aware of the 'phone ringing.

" Good morning dear boy, what's your news?"

"Ah, Leo Price," I acknowledged. "In a nut shell I've met this really tremendous girl, been to a million clubs dropped a trillion pills but on the down side I've just had to cancel a trip to Ibiza."

"Sounds a good job, don't want you overdoing it do we? Anyway tell me more about this woman, that's what I'm really interested in.

"Well she's tall, dark with long curly hair, cute and enjoys partying, you should meet her."

"Oh, no, no, I am far too busy to be socialising at the moment, just wanted to catch up on the news, have you anything else to tell me."

"No." I certainly wasn't going to tell him about our little experiment or anything else.

Oh well if there's nothing else, I shall be off, toodle pip."

I lent back and stretched. For some strange reason his 'phone calls kept me on my toes, there was something of the father, son, teacher, pupil feeling about it. He probably wouldn't bat an eyelid if I told him what I was really up to but some things really did have to remain totally confidential.

Embracing the Sunshine

Friday night was absolutely massive. James, Lewis, Greg, Graham, Jeff and myself had a really big night. We'd planned to go straight on to a huge out door party in Oxford as soon as the club finished. We'd all been looking forward to it for some time. It was the first decent licensed out door event of the year. Somehow during the course of the evening Lewis, Greg James and Graham dropped out. No stamina is what I'd say, or maybe not enough speed as the case maybe. A couple of us went back to my flat to catch a few hours sleep and then Summer, Jeff and myself took Graham to the tube station on our way out of London. He didn't feel up to it. Quite simply I didn't blame him he'd really freaked last night, instead of lifting him higher and higher his pill dropped him to basement level and we had to take it in turns to sit with him and reassure him that his world wasn't going to completely fall in. Anxiety and depression aside he had to pick his wife up from the airport at lunch time, she didn't know anything about the pills and there was no way that I wanted him to come to Oxford to try another in the hope that it would shift him in the right direction this time. He was better off giving it a totally wide berth and sticking with the beer or whatever agreed with him. E like anything else reacts differently with different people and he was best quitting while he was still ahead. The rest of them had a mixture of excuses

Embracing the Sunshine

ranging from work to family commitments. I don't think that they really knew what they were going to miss.

The closer we got to Oxford the better atmosphere. There were literally hundreds of cars going in the same direction. The traffic slowed to a walking pace on the narrow country lane leading to the site. Nobody was in the least bit bothered about this particular traffic jam, people jumped in and out of cars striking up conversations with total strangers comparing it to the nights when the M4 and M5 used to be blocked rave solid. There was a definite rave feeling of common purpose. It didn't really matter if the traffic didn't move another inch, we were all enjoying ourselves blasting out the countryside with DJ mix tapes. Jeff was in good spirits telling everyone about the motorway that he'd discovered running through the back room in the crowded club last night. He'd had to be really careful when he was dancing so as not to get run over but quite enjoyed the lights of the cars and lorries as they flashed past him. Sounded like there'd been some ketamine or acid in his E, whatever it was at least he had had a better time than Graham.

We gave a can of oil to a group of people standing round a car that needed just that little bit of engineering encouragement to get to its destination. The first view of the fields was awe inspiring. I didn't realise that they built tents so big. There was a Ferris wheel, fun fair and a huge open air area. I couldn't wait. I might not be going to Ibiza but I was going to really enjoy myself here. Even a group of local farmers walking against the general flow of the traffic were full of nothing but praise and bewilderment at the scale and quality of the temporary village that had sprung up over night.

It was so big that we decided that we'd have an on the hour every hour meeting point by a Moby billboard outside the biggest tent.

Jeff was frantically running round in vain trying to find someone to score some more pills. He needed sorting out, we left Summer talking to a group of people she'd met and went off to score him some Es. I was still had enough and Summer, well of course she didn't do things like that.

The security had been a lot tighter than the usual club frisks and I wondered whether we were going to find anything. I reassured myself that at a do like this there must be someone selling something even if its just the odd pill. We took forever to find anything though. It was just by the edge of one of the tents. Two young lads were acting very nervously. Not like the confident club dealers that I 'd noticed in London. Jeff was at the other end of the tent so I asked them what they had. Pills was the reply, not a brand name, just pills. I asked them to wait there whilst I got my mate.

"You're not the Police are you?" they asked nervously.

I reassured them and ran back to get Jeff. Miraculously they were still there when we got back. I stood aside and let him do the business transaction with them. They left and Jeff, said that he'd paid a tenner each for two, to compliment the one he still had from last night. He showed me the pills. One was misshapen and the other white and unmarked.

Embracing the Sunshine

My heart sank as he showed them to me. I should have done the checking myself. It was his first time face to face with a dealer and I'd forgotten how uneven the power equation feels when they've got something you want and you're not sure that you're going to get a better offer.

Mercifully he had a big one. We got split up soon after we got back to Summer and I didn't see him again until about nine am the next day.

Summer and I had a few beers in the afternoon, we decided to take it easy after all there were fifteen hours of party on offer and it seemed a shame to miss out on some of the out door events like the Mutant Waste tribal drumming sessions where everyone was invited to hit something in time with the drummers who were building up an awesome beat with their imaginative drums made out of all manner of found and reclaimed items.

I wasn't feeling up to the Ferris wheel so I let Summer go on that by herself. She had a wonderful time but there was no way that I was going up there not in a million years. The only highs I was interested in today were chemical ones and I wasn't going to pay for the pleasure of being flown upside down at fantastic heights. Still it was a great idea to have the fun fair there and it looked marvellous as the night progressed. It was a big reminder to everyone on the site and those for miles around that tens of thousands of people were having the time of their lives. Summer had her 'photo taken with a man wearing nothing but black, leather zip- up underpants and someone else with a bone through his nose. I'd never seen her as excited about anything. We talked briefly to a girl in a really cool dress which said, over and over again, "someday we'll all be free," Today perhaps, I thought, there were no rules, no restraints, just total unadulterated freedom and enjoyment.

I told Summer that I was going to drop my pill at about seven o'clock. I thought I'd better tell her or she might freak when she saw me getting more and more animated. What I hadn't bargained for was that she might want one herself. I was a little bit worried that she might have totally disapproved but no there was no stopping her when I introduced the subject. There was something about her that I never really understood. Beneath her straight exterior was an inquisitive, mischievous nature that excelled with the mere mention of something illicit. It was as if life was a game to her and that that there was no part too dangerous or off bounds. My concern was that she might not know how to apply the brakes.

"Can I have one? Can I have one?"

"No. No. No."

This went on forever. Literally forever.

I told her that Graham had experienced a bad trip last night. That didn't deter her.

I explained that even a half would be too strong for her. More over I told her that I didn't want to be responsible for getting her involved with drugs. It wasn't that there was anything wrong with ecstasy. I was sure of that. I suppose it was just that I felt responsible, paternalistic I suppose. I knew what the drug was like but it was all a matter of how she'd cope with the change in her values. I was aware of the cookie type of person she was meeting and if I was giving her the message that all drugs were okay then perhaps I was doing her a disservice. I told her as much.

She seemed to take it all on board and gave me reassurances to that effect, I wasn't entirely certain that she knew what she was getting involved with. I suppose that I relented and agreed that she could start off with a quarter to shut her up and to get a bit of peace. That was a mistake once she'd got her foot in the door there was no stopping her. At least I knew it was what she wanted.

"Well you're having a whole one it's not fair." She pleaded.

I hadn't bargained for such persistence. For the tenth time I repeated that, body weight, metabolism and tolerance through use meant that a whole pill would overtake her in the heat.

I eventually agreed to a half. Against my better judgement. I might not be afraid to tell people about the wonders of ecstasy, what pleasures I derived from it but I wasn't going to make anyone take it against their will. I wasn't going to push it.

As the evening progressed we found one of the quieter tents. When I say quieter, I mean one that still had room around the sides to sit and chill if necessary. There were still three or four thousand people in there. The heat had soaked the ceiling of the tent and the humidity was trickling down the canvas side walls it might not have been the typical, rave associated, muddy English field outside but the perimeters of the tent had already begun to cut up from the perpetual drips.

"Acid rain," I laughed as a drop hit me on the head.
"What?"

Embracing the Sunshine

"Acid rain as in Acid as in House as in rain." I explained to her.

Despite the wet ground we sat and chatted close to the edge of the inside of the tent, she was really excited about her first half. We took them together and I explained that it would probably take about half an hour to take effect. I didn't tell her about the initial queasy nauseous effect my first pill had on me. It was best to deal with difficulties if and when they arose and not to anticipate problems. I didn't want her to be too anxious so as not to be able to let herself get into it.

Fifteen minutes after I'd taken mine I felt a familiar E or speed related need to urinate. I had to go. I couldn't wait. I felt terrible about leaving her there but I had to go. I'd be back in time before she kicked in. "Five minutes," I explained.

"Be quick Baba." She purred affectionately

I left her with a Scottish lad who we'd been talking to earlier. I briefly explained what was happening. He'd look after her.

I rushed out into the night and the sounds of the other tents. The sun had gone down and the arena was lit by the moon and the whirring lights of the Ferris wheel. There was an infectious buzz about it all. I should have gone to the toilet right there outside the tent but the allure of the evening bustle compelled me to run through the crowds to the main toilets area.

I came straight back and had no difficulty in finding the entrance to the right tent. I retraced my steps. I remembered it was fifteen paces right and ten paces deep. She wasn't there. He wasn't there. They'd gone. I had no chance of finding them in the midst of thirty thousand people. They could be in any of the five tents, outside or on the fun fair. I had no idea. I'd just given someone I cared about her first E and I'd just lost her. She was probably coming up right now. He'd look after her wouldn't he? I'd no idea whether she'd like or not. It would probably be disastrous, she'd probably fret about me not being there, she'd end up in the hospital tent. I'd already lost Jeff and I felt bad enough about that. This was sheer torture.

I was coming up myself but I couldn't quite snap into it. I couldn't ignore the beats. I started to move. I racked my brains as to what to do but the clarity which often seemed to accompany a night on the pills had deserted me. Thinking was a muddled process which was becoming heavily loaded with self doubt.

Then it struck me. The DJ. podium was in the wrong position. I'd just come in through the wrong entrance to the marquee. I needed to be over the other side. There were five entrances but it had to be the one directly opposite. I started to move through the crowd but realised that it would be quicker to go out and come in again. I dashed round avoiding the clusters of people who were sitting out in the warm night air.

I found our Scottish friend, no problem. Summer wasn't there though.

"She's gone to the toilets. Just after you did. Should be back soon."

I thanked him and we began to dance. Deep down though I still felt sick. I hoped that she had better luck getting back than I did. there wasn't too much I could do about it. I just stayed and danced and hoped.

The jab in my ribs couldn't have come as a more welcome surprise.

"Where've you been? she bubbled."

Looking for you . You wouldn't believe..." I stopped myself, she was back and she was up. She'd reached that higher state of consciousness. I'd messed it up once and I wasn't going to do it again by running all my fears and concerns past her.

She was radiant, effervescent, bouncing, dancing and yelping. She made me feel an awful lot better. There was nothing that could beat being up and enjoying yourself with someone that you really cared for.

We exchanged whoops and gestures, with our Scottish friend. He was called Jerry as well. We danced forever, every time the strobes came on or the lights swept the area we were dancing in the whole tent seemed to be absolutely electric. We were firing on all cylinders with a chemically fuelled exuberance which couldn't be bettered.

Perhaps an hour or two later, Summer shouted in my ear," it's really cold in here."

"You're joking," I said, taking a sip from one of the two, two litre water bottles which we'd had with us all day and had threatened to make us the two most popular people at the party.

"Baba, I want to sit down for a bit, will you sit with me?"

Of course I would. I felt like dancing but if she wanted company then I was there for her. We sat on a black hooded top I'd brought in case we had to be outside. It stopped us from getting wet on the cold damp earth. At least she wasn't reacting too badly, I put it down to tiredness. She was happy to lie and sleep curled up in a ball as later I danced by her, carefully positioned so that no one would tread on her by accident as they moved around in the tent.

Scottish Jerry came over and asked whether we'd like to go outside for a while. He suggested a smoke, well she was cold and we didn't smoke but nonetheless it seemed a good idea. There was less chance of getting trodden on . We filed out through the animated crowd. There were six of us in all.

We all introduced ourselves, shook hands, sat down in a tight circle and I immediately forgot everyone's name apart from Jerry's of course. He seemed very much in control. Very much the leader. One of his friends gave Summer a back massage. Jerry explained to me that he'd moved down to the south coast ten years ago but that he was proud of his accent. He said it gave him a sense of identity in a sea of indifference as he put it.

Here, said Jerry, as he opened a pouch which he produced from underneath the front chest pockets of his dungarees. I saw that he was wearing a 'Klubbers, Nice Trippsies' tee-shirt that parodied the box of a well known breakfast cereal with an assortment of drugs being ladled out of a bowl by an eager clubber.

"If you don't smoke there must be something in here for you." Jerry showed us its contents saying "There's E's, whiz or strawberries."

He was just offering them there was no request for payment, most of these things were so expensive but he was just offering them to us like you'd offer to buy a round of drinks in the pub.

Summer wasn't in any fit state and I wasn't ready to take another one. I'd come right down but that was the best way at the moment I told myself. If she needed looking after I needed to be on the same planet.

"That's, okay mate just being sociable." He was.

Summers back massage was over. She seemed to be perking up a bit more.

"What do you do?"

"Accountancy and Personnel" I said referring to myself and Summer respectively

"I'm a drugs counsellor," he replied.

That helped even more, Summer giggled at this seemingly incongruous statement.

A bit of method acting" I quipped

He didn't laugh but showed me no sign of being perturbed.

"This is all separate, recreational, you know" He said in a matter of fact tone.

"What type of people do you deal with?" I asked somewhat intrigued.

"All sorts, but it's normally horse and whiz addicts"

"Whiz!", I was rather surprised.

"Oh! yeah! an awful lot of Whiz, too much whiz and you're up for ages, well, days everything goes quicker you feel better equipped to do things but when you are least expecting it. Bang, Crash. You hit the lowest of low, because that high, when your body makes you pay for it. Can't keep on going. Unless you are on Whiz that is. Most of them keep going right on until they need more and more of the stuff to even start the day. It is psychologically not physically addictive you know. I just use it to prolong my E. And most the crap these days is just speed. A purest would say Whiz adulterates the empathy you feel on E, but if there is no E to be adulterated I'm not exactly losing anything am I. Saying that I've had some really good pills tonight,"

"Yeah, same here," I replied.

I wasn't ready for anything other than E's and Poppers I didn't want to have anything to keep me going. Speed seemed a great idea to keep the weekend going but a real disaster if you needed to go to work.

Summer was back to cradling her head in my lap. More alert, friendly and enjoying rather than needing the attention. She joked with Jerry that it was her first E and that she had only taken it because her boyfriend was having one. At least she could see the funny side of it all.

Jerry told us all about Strawberries, well not Strawberry, Strawberries but the type that comes on a blotter. A tab of Lysergic Acid that is! I wasn't going any where near that after Tony's story.

"There is no way," I said, "I would even contemplate it, I was sure I would have a bad trip. Certain of it."

"All in the mind, a trip is a trip it is a psychological experience. It just depends on the state of mind, if you can change that from bad to good the trip changes as well. Mushrooms, Magic Mushrooms are better if you have not tripped before but I have not got any." He laughed. "Tripping just accentuates colour, shape and sounds, makes you happy giggling and gives you insight as to what is going on around you. There's no better way to have a good nights raving than on a trip, it's a real educational drug."

"Yeah, I've heard but I'll be sticking to the Es just now." I said aware of my incongruous yet entrenched conservatism on the issue.

"Come on," said Summer "I've got to go, we'll be back"

I went with her. She was amused by Jerry's occupation and told me that she felt slightly out of her depth in the group, slightly intimidated by the back massage and that she thought that it was all genuine but while there was a slight doubt in her mind, she'd like to move on.

She was really cold again and after the toilets we decided to go back to the car and get some more clothes. Unfortunately there was no re-admittance from the car park and neither of us felt like leaving this particular party just yet.

I had seen girls walking around with silver foil blankets wrapped around their shoulders. Cool I thought, the only other alternative was an antique hospital blanket from a store which was busy filling a gap in the market. No, they didn't look too wonderful and then I remembered the St John's Ambulance sign. We'd ask there, after all she was pretty cold and at three am it wasn't going to get any warmer in a hurry.

The lady at the admittance counter was friendly but fair. "You'll have to check in first and fill in this form."

We both looked at each other. We weren't sure about that, there was no way they we wanted our names and addresses recorded.

"But, she only needs a blanket"

"Even so, you will have to check her in." Well we would have to anyway.

"What's wrong with you?" asked the girl at the admissions desk.

"Cold, very cold" I answered for her.

"Seems to be a lot of that tonight. Either too hot or too cold" she replied in a friendly manner.

"Can I come through as well to keep her company?" I asked.

"Yes, you better take a seat down there."

We walked down a canvass tunnel to a row of chairs. And sat amongst the other minor casualties. A young uniformed attendant joined us. Chirpily he asked "Well, what is the matter with you two?

"It is her, she is too cold"

He checked her brow with the back of his hand and agreed with me. "Yes she's very cold, before I can do anything else I'll have to get the nurse."

By this time I'd taken off my shirt and given it to Summer, to cover her modest top.

Within moments a nurse breezed calmly and efficiently up to the pair of us. "Right , which one of you is too cold?" she asked without even a hint of irony. I could tell that she wasn't being cynical, just professional. After all the fact that I didn't have a shirt on could have just as easily have suggested that I was the one who was cold.

"We'll have to find you a stretcher to lie on." She said to Summer.

"But cannot we just have one of those nice silver blankets? pleaded Summer

Embracing the Sunshine

"No, you're very, very cold. You've lost an awful lot of heat. I'd compare that with running a couple of marathons. You're free to walk out of here but I wouldn't like it if you did."

Summer didn't need too much encouragement to lie on the stretcher. She was first covered by one of the coveted silver blankets and then by a conventional woollen one. I cleared it with the nurse before lying next to her on the stretcher. I'd be able to give her a bit of extra warmth and reassurance.

"Chill out room, I joked to myself, I've found the chill out room."

The young volunteer, David I think his name was, came over and checked her again after about half an hour. She was still very cold and had fallen asleep. He asked me to wake her for him. It was important that she didn't get too hot and sweaty from the foil blanket. I helped roll her over. She didn't like that at all. Her small hands put up quite a fight as I tried to wrestle the silver foil blanket away from her. She wasn't giving up that easily. We won despite the protests, rolled her over and let her settle back into a deep sleep.

She was a picture of serenity. She appeared happy and safe. I was missing the music but at least I could sit and chill with her. There'd be time for dancing before the night was over.

There was a constant flow of visitors to my chill out area. Boyfriends and girlfriends looking after each other. Sometimes it was groups bringing in bedraggled individuals. Thankfully there were no serious casualties. Most were like the nurse had said earlier, too hot or too cold, those rushing too much and those who hadn't had enough to drink.

A tall attractive girl, all arms and legs, wearing a fluffy, flimsy pink bikini, noisily entered the tent. She nonchalantly protested, "I'm all right, I am just really rushing, I don't know how many I've had but its loads, if you'd asked the boys I was with before they'd be able to tell you. They had more than me, all I want to do is dance but I'd like to have a seat for a bit."

"That wouldn't be too bad an idea now would it." said the nurse. Our new star attraction agreed .

As she sat her self down at the other end of the tent, she looked over and shouted hello to me. We exchanged names and the normal E disinhibited pleasantries and as a crowd gathered around her, she shouted across. "Jerry, they're putting me on a heart monitor, Jerry I've never been on a heart monitor before, are they any good? I'm on a heart monitor and all I want to do is dance."

"If I was you I'd just try to lie back and enjoy it for a while, you never know how long it'll be before you're on one again and it'd make sense to enjoy it while you're on it." I tried to encourage her.

I sat and watched her arms and legs going ten to the dozen. I hoped that she was all right. At least she'd got this far before anything serious could happen. She was beautiful, all of twenty one and on a heart monitor.

Our conversation was interrupted by some new arrivals. The doctors I am sure would have been glad of getting her undivided attention. Three young lads, perhaps sixteen or so took a chair next to our stretcher. Two of them were out of it and the third well he was rushing, really rushing. He sat on the chair framed by his friends, hunched forward, arms shaking head and legs jittering. His cheeks were flushed, his pupils the size of dinner plates. He puffed and puffed as if to keep a pace of himself.

Stating the obvious, I said, "You're really rushing there mate, how many have you had?"

"Seven, mate, seven good ones."

I was taken aback. I'd be completely out of it after three or four but seven, that seemed over doing it a bit, rather like going to the pub underage and getting absolutely smashed. It seemed to be missing the entire point of taking an E. Who knows maybe I was just getting too old for all of this, maybe that was the point of it all. Perhaps it was just all about what you wanted to do and we've all got different agendas. I was convinced myself that moderation was the best policy, later that Summer, after a friend ended up in St Mary's on a drip after a half dozen or so pills and twice as many pints on a hot afternoon at the Notting Hill Carnival

"We've been in the jungle tent." He panted like a racing commentator.

That explained it, those beats are anything from 140 -200 BPM.

"Too fast for me," I replied.

"Nah, it's the best, we're off to Sweat in Camden tonight." He meant it, probably wouldn't come down before then, I thought." They discharged themselves after a while. Peace had returned for a while, even my friend on the heart monitor had calmed down. I met someone in there who I was sure that I knew. She was half my age and we didn't go to the same clubs but I was sure that I knew her from somewhere. So was she but we couldn't work it out.

A group of reassuringly older looking lads came in. They were looking after a friend who was a barrister or a solicitor, he was totally off his trolley, too much speed according to his friends. We all had a real laugh when we discovered that we were all accountants. We decided to keep in touch, after all the proportion of E heads in the profession had to below that of the general population.

There was a friendly camaraderie in the tent. No one was seriously ill. Outside assistance wasn't required. Our chill out area lacked a lot of the characteristics of late night weekend casualty wings. There were no broken bones, no slashed faces and no violent outbursts. Ecstasy's problem though, is that it emits a glamour which the press won't ignore. It doesn't cause as much damage as alcohol or cigarettes but it demands the front pages of our papers. There was no logical reason for it. It was just another drug, a safer one than those which we'd legalised but as long as it remained forbidden that was to remain hidden from the public knowledge. Half of society seemed to see drugs as existing in two categories. Legal and illegal. The other half seeing them as being harmless soft drugs and harmful hard drugs. These divisions normally reflected age and upbringing, those factors themselves being a reflection of the general sea change which the UK had experienced in the last ten years since the floods of heroin to our council estates changed the conception that drugs were only for a very small minority of people. Drugs weren't just for losers, no far from it.

Embracing the Sunshine

I left Summer for a while. There were plenty of people who would look after her. The sun was coming up. What a glorious sight. Thousands of people dancing outside the tents rejoicing in the beginning of another beautiful day. There were still thousands inside the huge marquees. I ran over to the loudest, central tent, it was absolutely enormous, the largest tent that I'd ever seen, decked out with futuristic inflatables and the stage was washed in a battery of strobe lights. It had emptied out but saying that there were still at least five thousand in there. It was absolutely throbbing. I stayed for fifteen to twenty minutes, geared up by Carl Cox and the M.C, well if I'm honest I was fired up by Carl Cox, I couldn't quite understand why we had to have someone talking a frantic load of nonsense over his incredible music. I wanted to see Paul Oakenfold so I dashed over to another tent. As I was getting there the strains of his Perfecto mix of Reach Up by the Perfecto All Stars flooded across the busy field. I remembered the original version of Pig Bag by Pig Bag, but Oakeys mix was the best. I struggled to get through the entrance of the tent it was absolutely mobbed. He was rocking the crowd like I've never seen a crowd rocked before. I got right back into it and the vibe was awesome. Reluctantly, but faithfully I made my way back to the St John's Ambulance Chill Out Zone. Summer was still asleep but somehow I could tell by the contented look on her face that she was ready for the trip back home.

"It's time to get up." I said conscious that the event would soon be over.

"Just four more seconds."

119

Embracing the Sunshine

"Come on." I encouraged her

"Four more minutes." She resisted.

"No, come on it's officially over in half an hour and we'd better be prepared for the rush. Even the people here have got to get home haven't they?"

"No baba, just cuddle me, four more minutes."

It was only the promise of the return of her shiny silver rave blanket which eventually got her moving.

"Can I keep it? Really!" She exclaimed as if someone had given her a pair of Technics SL 1200s.

The staff confirmed that she was okay to leave. I thanked them all and said good-bye to everyone I still recognised there. My friend in the fluffy bikini had gone but I was assured that she was all right.

Summer wandered out of the tent and into the bright sunshine. She rubbed her eyes as I held her silver blanket round her shoulders. I held it at arms length and she wandered in a daze still rubbing her eyes with her telephone wire black curls flowing out and over the shiny silver that reflected the morning sun. Even amongst the eclectic non judgmental crowd she stuck out and was the centre of a few friendly chuckles and admiring comments. It took us two hours to find the car and another four hours to drive it off the site. The single track road couldn't cope with the sheer volume of traffic. We almost lost faith with the masses at one stage when we couldn't find the car, the idea that it had been stolen by anyone of the wonderful people that we'd shared the evening with was somewhat beyond comprehension and we both burst out laughing when we realised that we'd spent so long looking in the wrong field.

Embracing the Sunshine

Jeff got back to us half way through the morning. He wanted to know if we'd seen the parachutists, we hadn't and joked that he must have had taken some wicked pills. Apparently there had been some sort of a parachute display, heavens knows why it wasn't as if we needed any more entertainment at this stage of the day, besides it could positively give you a fright if you were coming down and all of a sudden people started to drop out of the sky around you.

It was the one of the hottest days of summer so we just sat around on the grass. Just about every car had a sound system of some description. Everyone just lay out in the open-air soaking up the sun and chilling to the DJ mix tapes.

I was fascinated by a couple in a battered Volvo Estate next to us. He'd been asking round for strawberries and eventually they lay down on the grass by us. They had a pill and a blotter each and they were lost in each other with no recognition of the crowds around them as they cuddled and caressed, disappearing into the morning after a while and we were left by ourselves taking in the still vibrant atmosphere of the unofficial after party.

Jeff had, had a good one, that was a real relief. For months later people came up to him in the street and in clubs, even when he had his suit on and told him that they recognised him from the Oxford party. Out of all us, apart perhaps from myself he had got the most out of the entire scene, the music, the clubs and the very rational of everything that was happening. Lots of people had even seen him on the BPM TV coverage. I'd videoed that myself and I can confirm that he was completely out of it, trancing it up to the sounds of Billy Nasty. He was there totally pilled out of it, with hamster cheeks and satellite dish eyes but it was definitely him, we ribbed him about it for ages joking how we should get a copy for his colleagues and clients at work. None of that mattered we'd all had a wonderful weekend. The promoter had been on TV to say that he wanted to put on a night that people would remember for the rest of their lives. He'd come very close.

I don't know how I stayed awake during the drive back to London, I was overtierd when I got back but was glad of a call from Leo Price. Apart from saying that whilst he didn't want to sound pejorative that he assumed that I hadn't lasted the weekend on beer alone. He wasn't really interested in my fantastic stories and I listened intentively as he told me how he'd had to fight off the attentions of a friends nanny who'd tried to get him in to bed when his children were playing with her charges in the next room. She'd been somewhat perturbed at his rejection and rang him later at four in the morning. This had caused ructions in the household, he told his wife that it was just a school girl with a crush on him, which of course was the truth. His wife took a lot of convincing and Leo said that he wouldn't have minded being hung for something that he'd actually done.

Can You Feel It

Can you Feel it

Friday night and Steve was no where to be seen, I'd looked round the club for ages but he definitely wasn't there. I found out why uncomfortably early the next morning. I fumbled for the telephone as I emerged from a deep sleep. The tones of the cracking mobile sounded as bad as I felt. "Hi, Jerry, it's Steve here," an aggressive white noise attacked and obscured his next line of conversation. The line went dead several times before he was able to tell me that he'd been tipped off not to go to London last night but most of his friends hadn't been that lucky. The Police had stopped them carrying hundreds of pills on the motorway. He wanted me to meet him, I didn't really know what I could do to help but I liked Steve and it would have destroyed me to see him pulled in on serious charges. We agreed to meet somewhere neutral in the deserted City square mile.

I probably looked awful after getting hardly any sleep but not as bad as Steve. The colour was drained from his cheeks and he was obviously petrified by last nights events. He told me story over and over again, he knew that his mates had been watched by the Police and thought that he was next on their list. We sat in his car a battered old Escort with blacked out windows. They weren't actually blacked out as such it was just that they were covered in a thick layer of cigarette smoke. Steve said that there was a reason for that and showing a brief return of his customary confidence, he lifted himself out of his gloom, explaining he didn't want to draw attention to his car. With a childlike enthusiasm he showed me the stereo system in the back of the car. The boot was full of speakers which wouldn't be out of place in most clubs. He cranked it up for a couple of seconds and the sub sonic bass of Joey Beltram's, 'Energy Flash' seemed to shake the buildings around us. I joked that we were trying not to draw attention to ourselves. We drove round the city chatting for a while, I arranged to put the rest of Steve's pills and his stash of cash into my safety deposit box. There was no way that he could deal at the moment.

Now there was a real urgency about making our own pills, what with Steve out of circulation the only prospect of getting a buzz was through buying dodgy pills off complete strangers. When the day actually came it felt like nothing else that I'd ever done before, it was the most ridiculous, dangerous, exhilarating thing I'd done in my life. My central, spacious and expensively decorated flat was rapidly being transformed into a factory. A drugs factory. A Class A drugs factory at that. The walls floor and ceiling of the kitchen were covered in black polythene and masking tape. Glass wear snaked its way around the sparse modernist, open plan kitchen. A mass of complex equipment stood ominously close to the extractor fan. Empty beakers and jars containing brightly coloured chemicals were carefully arranged on a collapsible table which Lewis had brought to give us more work space.

If anyone walked in now, that was it. Five years, ten years, fifteen years, who knows. Not worth thinking about I told myself. that's not going to happen, we're organised and smart enough to get through this, come

Can You Feel It

Monday lunch time we'd have the flat back to normal. The polythene would be burned. The glassware would be washed and rinsed several times in hot soapy water and baked for a couple of hours at 400 degrees and then quietly returned to Lewis's laboratory. All used containers would have their labels removed be smashed and put in the lift shaft of one of the other Barbican blocks.

The heat would be off us and we'd have a quarter to a third of a pound of very valuable little crystals. Little grains of love. Grains of love and money. I'd have made a healthy return on the investment of my time and to boot we'd have good ecstasy to impart on a market where good gear was getting harder and harder to find. Some surveys had found that for example out of twenty pills bought at clubs that only a couple of them actually contained any MDMA. Perhaps their researchers stood out as researchers and dealers knowingly sold them duds. I'd been lucky in what I'd bought so far but I didn't doubt that there was a lot of rubbish for sale out there. We'd be above that, we'd be the Marks and Spencers of the drug world.

We were largely in Lewis' hands. He had the knowledge and the expertise. James and I were there mainly for moral support. To keep him going and to perform ancillary duties. He was deep in his work explaining what we were actually going to do. "First of all we need a substituted Allybenzene which we're going to get from calamus. We could get it from quite a lot of different herbs, for example dill, nutmeg or sassafras but you know why we're not using sassafras. Basically it would be easier to start off with the real thing but of course what we need isn't legally available. If you want to know, an Allybenzene is a cojugated ring of six carbon atoms. The starting blocks are found in most of the aromatic compounds including the ones that I've just mentioned.

James and I sat fascinated, though not necessarily understanding exactly what he was saying.

He continued, "By the way doe anyone know what an E-Layer is?

"Well I suppose I'm going to in a minute." said James.

"It's a layer of the ionosphere able to reflect medium frequency waves." trumped Lewis

"That's a joke is it? Queried James.

"Doesn't seem right to me," I said, "when was the last time that you heard good E music on Medium Wave, no I think that the laws of physics or the Broadcasting Laws should be changed so that good F.M. E music and only E music is played through the E layer"

Lewis continued to paraphrase the procedure he was going to follow over the weekend. I'd read over most of it when I had blitzed my way through the books. All that had really taught me was that we needed to be patient and precise, there was no rushing things and second best wasn't good enough far any part of the process.

"Do any of you two have drug testing at work, like they do at London Underground?" Asked Lewis.

"No but there are days when I feel like testing a few drugs at work," replied James

"Seriously, if they give you warning about testing, E should be out of the system within three days but it helps to drink lots of water or beer to swill it out, it leaves the body almost exclusively through fluids, not like cannabis which stays in the system for ages." said Lewis.

"In that case I am tapping in to the drains at a club next week and I am going to distil and refine what comes out of there, that'll be quicker than being locked away here for the weekend." I joked.

"Rather you than me," said Lewis, "seriously if you get drug tested on the spot, apparently you can subvert the results by keeping a small bit of powdered bleach under your thumb nail, the bleach destroys any trace of amphetamine related substances but doesn't alter the test in any other way."

"I think at the moment that we're okay because none of us are suspected of any of this stuff at work and until we are then the problems not going to arise, I mean to say if the company just tested everyone across the board with no warning then there'd be a lot of crap flying about, they're not going to do that are they? I said.

"Is she dead yet?" enquired James

"Who?" I questioned.

"That girl in the news who collapsed on her pill." replied James.

"Yeah, yesterday, the papers were full of it, you couldn't miss it." said Lewis.

"Thank God, it was awful, I mean to say I thought that there was nothing else going on in the world. When was the last time that a drink-drive death, the death of a heroin addict or an alcoholic made the front page in even the local paper?" said James

"Someone said that it was speed and not E, certainly not a dodgy E and that she'd been drinking" I said.

"Yeah but that doesn't really matter does it, the papers were just looking for a story, it was the same with those kids up North, what you heard on the grapevine was a million times different to what you read. Lewis said.

"Its just a chance to sell newspapers and create what they used to call moral panics in the seventies." said James.

"You're showing your age," joked Lewis

"Look who's talking," James replied,

"It's all out of proportion isn't it, this girl and all that, I mean to say that she was probably a great person and all that and its a tragedy that she's died but it isn't going to stop anyone from taking E is it? It certainly isn't stopping us here cooking chemicals all weekend and I wouldn't put us down as the biggest bunch of callous ruthless cynics in the world. We'll have to be careful though you can make a sure bet that the up shot of this is that the Police will be working overtime to make a few token arrests, we're not going to provide them with the fodder for that." I said.

"Yeah, too right I was reading the Times Law Reports the other day and the Court of Appeal doesn't recognise that there are any differences between pills and smack. They're both Class A drugs as far as they are concerned, absolutely ridiculous," said Lewis.

There wasn't much to do, Lewis did literally all of the chemical work and James got the jitters every time that a helicopter flew over head. I had to constantly reassure him that it was nothing to do with our activities and just a fact of life living so close to the city. Lewis brightened things up by telling us that his senior partners had been away for an executive weekend and that come the early hours of the morning when they were battling it out on the snooker table they'd run out of chalk. Apparently one of the more senior members had just got a large lump of cocaine, a part of the block, so to speak and had rubbed down the cues with it.

We got through the tedium of being cooped up by discussing how we were going to get rid of the pills. James wondered what we should call them, he was in favour of Black Diamonds, he'd been out with Claire once and he tried to buy some pills off a big chap who happened to be black. He was told that they were diamonds and hadn't heard of these before so he went back to tell Claire all about it. What he actually told her it all got mixed up in the translation and she spent ages talking to her friends trying to find out whether anyone had heard of black diamonds. Of course they hadn't and quite a buzz was generated by the discovery of what was thought to be a new type of pill.

James had looked into getting rid of the pills and there was a consensus of agreement that we'd have to set up our own club night. Of course there were hundreds of them in London and the surrounding areas. We had the disadvantage of not really knowing anyone on the scene but that wasn't going to get in our way after all we had goods to sell and we were determined to do it. The boys were keen to put on a house night but London was really packed to the gills with those. They weren't too keen on my suggestion that we play it harder and go for pure techno in a big way. I tried to convince them that it was the only way forward and that the listings always had a dearth of techno on a Saturday night. We were all decided though that whatever we were going to do wasn't going to be in the average run of the mill club, we didn't want problems with the in-house drug dealing system and to fill up the place and only line the pockets of other people. No we wanted to find somewhere big that we could easily and cheaply convert and get a licence for.

I'd been aware of a large disused bus station quite near Victoria. It had a hanger sized ground floor and from what I could make out the basement was just as extensive I'd look into that, see who owned it and canvass the idea with them. It wasn't Leicester Square but we didn't have to rely too much on passing trade if we had a big name specialist night on. Lewis suggested that there could be some huge unused office buildings in the City but we decided that most of them were probably being used as temporary office accommodation since the IRA bomb had caused so much devastation and in any event the increased security in the City wouldn't take too kindly to being overwhelmed by wave after wave of all night clubbers.

We were going to have to use all of the free publicity available. Everything from Mixmag, Muzik, Eternity, DJ, The Face, Arena, Time Out, NME, Melody Maker, The National Press, local radio, local TV anywhere that would give us a plug. James would go round personally to see the people responsible, we had to get ourselves known as we had no track record. We had to let people know that we knew what we were about. Then there were the posters and fliers. I'd look into getting those printed and we'd have to fly post some of those ourselves. Most club nights seemed to rely on word of mouth and fliers, well, we were going to fly post our way into peoples heads.

We'd have to plan in advance, those top DJs really do get quite busy. I'd read a Jeremy Healy interview and when he was asked what he thought he'd be doing in five years time he couldn't say because he didn't have his diary with him. Obviously he was joking only just. The day dragged on and it got worse as the evening approached. We all wanted to go out and do something. The Television was awful and we couldn't agree on a video to watch. I'd planned that we could all take it in turns on a rota basis to get some sleep but James and I just sat and lazed while Lewis kept a close eye on what he was doing. I don't know how Lewis kept on going, perhaps it was just the sheer responsibility of it. He was the driver who had to stay awake and we were the passengers nodding off after the first leg of the journey.

I suggested that we could go to The Final Frontier for a couple of hours to break the monotony. Anything to break the tedium of being cooped up in the flat, we could be 'drug free clubbers' as I put it.

James was up for the idea but Lewis insisted that we were staying put, there was no way that we were going to be drug free clubbers, we were going to be 'club free druggies' as he put it. Even when we ran out of coffee Lewis insisted that I didn't go out for any. He wanted us all to be around just in case there were any problems.

Can You Feel It

Eventually after he'd reached the end of a particular stage he agreed to come out with us and take a break. We only went to a local corner shop and waited in the Pizza Delivery Shop to take delivery of our own Pizzas. The shop assistant was adamant that we should go home and that he'd have it delivered within twenty minutes but Lewis was the more obdurate, he didn't want anyone coming in a million miles of the flat even if it was only to the door step with a couple of Pizzas. James made a few jokes about takeaway drugs mentioning a chip shop in Manchester which was raided after offering a little bit more than salt and vinegar with its fish and chips.

We all benefited from the short break but all in all Saturday evening was as bad as Friday. Come Sunday evening things were going really slow inducing somnolence in one and all. Lewis had just refiltered a process which we were supposed to have done on Saturday evening. It was going to take longer than expected, but Lewis wasn't able to say yet just how much longer. I was lazing on the sofa. Playing with the remote controls. One hand was flicking through the ceefax pages the other fiddling with the c.d. trying to find the break in Chemical Beats by the Chemical Brothers. I was forced to drop both of them and throw myself to the floor.

A large crash emanated from the kitchen. It wasn't like a bomb, no I'd felt what one of those was like, this place had jumped at least a good two inches when the I.R.A. bomb had gone off in Broadgate. No this wasn't that serious. But it was for me. Lewis was screaming, "Cover your faces," as he grabbed a cushion and ran towards the

Can You Feel It

French windows which he flung open. He gasped in the purer city air, yelling "get out here, get out here on the balcony."

We didn't need that much encouragement. James was panicking. "I'm off that's it I've had enough you could have bloody killed us."

"Just, fucking shut up! Now!" Lewis dictated sternly swiftly bundling James out of the window with him.

I knew that it was all over. Two and a half days. Two and a half solid days of slog and patience down the drain or down my bloody walls to be precise." No chance of scrapping it all off and starting again," I said trying to make light of the situation.

Lewis didn't really have to answer but said, "No way, now that it's oxygenated its worthless and more to the point its probably toxic and quite possibly deadly. There's a good chance that the reactions created Hydrogen Cyanide. That's the reason we're out here."

I might have given a lot of thought as to what we'd do with the rewards from our operation and rationalised the risks of getting caught but I hadn't really gone through the possibilities of it all going wrong. After all I'd trusted Lewis, it was his business, he had all of the books, all of the equipment and the benefit of up to date information from the internet. No this shouldn't have happened, but it had. I had to get used to that.

Lewis said that he thought that it had been a problem with the glassware, that he wasn't sure whether one of the piping joints was properly closed.

"Never mind the bloody glassware," said James, sitting on the floor looking totally destroyed. "What are we going to do surely someone must have heard that." He had a point.

"Well we can't go back in, that'd far too dangerous we don't know what's blowing round," Lewis said in a serious tone.

"It's a long shot but what about climbing along the outside of the balconies and hoping that we can disappear through an open window. I'm sure that we could find a flat where they've gone out and left their windows open. I do it all the time You wouldn't expect intruders at this height." I bit my lip, here I was on my own balcony, sheltering from the shattered remnants of an ecstasy factory and I was suggesting that we all risk our necks climbing from balcony to balcony breaking and entering into my neighbours flats.

Lewis seemed to think that it was an excellent idea. "Great, its our only option, if that stuff is toxic we'll cop it any way if we stay here for too long. It's move or nothing there are no other options. When we leave we'll leave the doors open, shouldn't take more than a couple of hours to dissipate the fumes, it'll be safe enough to go in with a face mask and turn on that extractor fan full blast, and clean up the remnants."

Now I was going to expose my neighbours to the fumes as they were emitted. What the hell had I got myself into. This should be the province of the big boys with proper premises and better thought plans. Well actually it would be far safer if it performed legally within the Health and Safety provisions. I didn't have time to cogitate further as I literally had to pull James behind me, he'd completely lost it. I didn't blame him. The idea of walking on ten inch ledges high above the City wasn't the most alluring of prospects at any time. James took just two steps and slipped. He lurched forward, twisted and somehow had the forethought to hurl his body back towards the balcony, he'd almost gone. Sweating, protesting and absolutely petrified we coaxed him back onto the ledge where he shuffled along clinging on for dear life.

Somehow we managed it. I dreaded the thought of anyone looking out of their windows or worse still sitting out on their balconies. It was still warm enough for that. I suppose we could have said that we'd had a chip pan fire or something, we certainly looked too shook up to be regular burglars.

We made it to the third flat along which I knew was empty. Lewis used a credit card to open it, "Look away," he said making light of the situation, "I don't want anyone to suggest that I've been teaching you all bad habits!"

The front door had a mortise lock and no key so we had to go out of a window that faced out on to the external walkway. Lewis suggested that James get himself a taxi home as he didn't look up to the cleaning up operation. He was off like a flash.

It was only after he'd left and I was standing there in shorts and a tee-shirt that I realised that I'd left my keys in the flat. We couldn't risk the balcony a second time and there was no way that I was going to draw any further attention to ourselves by trying it break down the front door.

Can You Feel It

Lewis was calm beyond the call of duty. He nonchalantly suggested that we drive back to his Docklands flat. He was right when he suggested that I'd have a spare set of keys to the flat in my drawer at work. We couldn't risk going there tonight and besides I didn't have my security pass. We'd have to do this first thing in the morning when the regular security were there . They knew me. He'd lend me a suit and we'd both go back and clear the place up. Lewis said that as no one had turned up at my flat yet that if anyone had heard anything that they cannot have thought it serious enough to investigate or call the emergency services. Our only problem would be burglars and considering the admirable security at the Barbican that was highly unlikely. It would defy all the realms of probability to have two sets of people climbing over those balcony rails in one evening.

Lewis suggested that we should have stuck to cocaine, if we'd invested as much thought and effort into smuggling some of that from Cartagena, where he'd been on holiday then we'd be rich men. He went on to say that the mark up on the streets over here was two hundred times what it was sold for over in Colombia. He said that the best thing about cocaine and the reason why it was so expensive was that as well as buying what you got, you were paying for what you didn't get, that is the after effects associated with other drugs. If cocaine was £60 a gram on the streets at the moment that meant that, on Lewis' calculations £60 could buy you two hundred grams in Cartagena. That was a very attractive prospect, but E was what I was really interested in and the poetic lure of Cartagena, tropical paradise and all had to be seen in the ruthless light of the gun totting cocaine barons who operated over there. It wasn't only cocaine that was cheap, life was cheap in Cartagena.

We went out to Brick Lane and picked up a take away. The sooner all of those restaurants got delivery services the better I thought. We sat and watched T.V. His girlfriend wasn't back until Tuesday, gone to her parents or something so we wouldn't have to explain why I needed somewhere to stay. We could have used the chip pan excuse but I was getting tired of telling lies to people, I much preferred the open, honest, unreserved ecstasy inspired state. It was ironic that we had to lie and scheme to achieve it. If E was legal we wouldn't have been here in the first place.

Not for the first time I'd gone back to the flat expecting to see the drug squad there. It was pretty much as we'd left it but there was a refreshing feeling about being back home and knowing that everything was getting back to normal. Lewis did a quick chemical check before letting me over the threshold of my own front door. I was surprised at how little mess there was. Lewis vacuumed and shampooed the chemical dregs. Amazingly the wooden floor and the marble work surfaces were intact, as was the bulk of the glassware, bar two of the glass beakers and their connecting pipes. Lewis said that this confirmed what he'd mentioned yesterday about the connections not fitting properly. On his analysis of what could have happened we had got away very lightly. He insisted that all of the equipment and the vacuum cleaner were best disposed of, we wouldn't be able to do this again. It wasn't that we couldn't refine our process to function properly, it was just that as a group we weren't mentally prepared for it and it was best to get out whilst the going was good. He was right. I'd known this since yesterday but I felt a twinge of sorrow of unfulfilled ambition as we agreed to call an end to our operations.

Lewis could see that I was upset, and he reassured me saying that this was a game for the big boys and that the biggest mistake we'd made was starting in the first place. He joked that at least next weekend we could go out and have a big one without any fears of a criminal record for producing ecstasy.

I smiled and joked that all they could get us for was a conspiracy or an attempt to produce a Class A drug."

"On yesterdays showing that would be a conspiracy to commit the ridiculous." Lewis joked and we agreed that we'd better ring James to see how he was coping with all of last nights excitement.

"Did you see the colour of his cheeks, when we were going over those balconies? I hope that he's resisted the temptation to talk to anyone about all of this." said Lewis

James wasn't talking to us. He was obviously still in shock but at least he was at work. If he'd have told Claire then half of London would know. He obviously hadn't and I knew how he operated, tomorrow it would all be forgotten as if it hadn't happened. It would become the source of joke, after joke in the future.

That was it, the reality was that we weren't going to be able to produce our own ecstasy. That had been clear from the minute that the apparatus had exploded. It should have been clear from the moment that I'd realised that this wasn't the same as making a cup of tea or baking a cake. It was a compound and not a mixture and as such it put it out of the reach of me and for that matter out of the hands of the non practising chemist like Lewis. The stupid thing was that I still had this yen to make it and for the rest of the week I racked my brains and scoured the web sites on the internet hoping for a breakthrough in the method of production. I convinced myself that there must be an easier way, I remembered the news clipping I'd taken about a group who'd made it in a microwave in a flat in East London, surely they were just using the microwave to do some of the heating processes that we had done with a Bunsen burner? Well it didn't say in the paper and from what depressing news I was able to find on the internet it appeared that my dream had indeed gone up in smoke. I wasn't going to bestow upon the world a great advance in organic chemistry and ecstasy was going to continue to be something I bought and not made.

The week really dragged. I gave Steve a ring I was conscious that I hadn't had time to return his calls. I'd been too tied up in what I was doing. He'd had his own problems. Jules had left him, she'd lost interest when he'd stopped dealing, she missed the buzz of it the money and the qudos it all brought, all of her mates would have died to have a dealer for a boyfriend. She'd found someone else and there was nothing that he could do to persuade her to come back. I didn't try to tell him that in those circumstances perhaps she wasn't worth it, no he didn't need to know that. The new boyfriend was into drugs in a big way, made Steve look like a small time player. Even if Steve went back dealing he wouldn't be able to compete and anyway things were getting pretty hot for him, there'd been an anonymous telephone call saying that there was a knife or worse ready for him if he was seen working in the wrong place in the future.

I suggested to him, hypothetically, of course, that if someone was planning to set up a large one off, monthly club would he be interested in controlling the pills side of the business. Well I didn't need to ask, of course he would, he had the skill the experience and he wasn't getting too much joy being unemployed so to speak.

I told him that a friend of mine was thinking about something like this and that if it came up that I'd make sure that Steve's c.v. was on the top of the pile. He thought that he should be able to keep his nose clean enough in the mean time for the Police to lose interest in him following the arrest of his mates. His only worry was what was going to happen next week when the Court found out that his friends hadn't kept their bail and could be anywhere from here to Hong Kong and back.

He suggested that we meet for a couple of beers that evening down his neck of the woods. His brothers club had Graham Gold doing a mid week slot. I wasn't too keen on going, if the Police were keeping an eye on Steve then I wasn't sure whether it was a good idea for me to be seen out there in the sticks with him. Didn't matter I thought, no one would be any clearer as to who I was it was along way out of London and I wasn't going to stick out from the crowd if I had my clubbing clobber on.

Steve's brothers Club was a breath of fresh air. The crowd might have been younger, some of them still had white gloves and white anti radiation masks, reminiscent

Can You Feel It

of Altern 8. There were a couple of fluorescent orange jackets, with slogans like, "Drugs Squad" and "Narcotic Enforcement" emblazoned on the back. At least they had a sense of humour. Everyone was really friendly and I suppose that here everyone really did know everyone. Graham Gold was awesome. You might not find this Goldie in every ones list of top DJs but he ripped the place apart, he played what the crowd wanted and it certainly wasn't sweet sickly hand bag, this was music that got harder, tunes which were mixed up with surprises thrown in. Quite simply it was one of the best house sets that I've heard.

The club closed early, probably about two o'clock I should have gone straight back to London but Steve persuaded me to join him and a group of friends on a trip down to the beach. He said that we'd watch the sun come up but I wasn't sure that I could justify staying that long.

I was glad that I stayed. I hadn't realised how beautiful the Kent coast was. We found our way to a cove cut off from the nearest hint of civilisation. One of the cars doubled as a sound system, the boot was raised to expose a huge set of sub woofer car speakers which enriched the morning air with resonating rhythmic bass. A camp fire was established close to the high water mark, it acted as a focal point, people dancing or sitting as the mood dictated.

I felt really invigorated, I could see the moon and the stars, I was sitting directly on terra firma and the sea lapped reassuringly on to the beach. I took off my shoes to feel closer to the earth, feeling the soft sand run through my toes as I danced. I felt an integral part of

141

everything around me and dancing was the key that opened up the path to environmental unity.

Work was the last thing on my mind, but I had to go, Steve had the same problem so I gave him a lift and sped in the direction of London hoping to miss the early morning queues of soulless, sad eyed commuters .

I got back in time to grab a shower, there were messages on the machine, Summer wanted me to ring her, Lewis wanted to talk to me about the promotion plans, was I playing football on Sunday and what were we going to do at the weekend? None of it really seemed to matter I was only gradually coming down from the shamanic vibrancy of the night before and quite frankly nothing was going to interrupt the melodic mantra which was mellowly washing around my head.

Friday we decided to go to a house event at one of the more celebrated London venues, which was incongruously set in the otherwise desolate wasteland north of Kings Cross. It was just three of us, Summer Jeff and I. We'd all made a real effort dress wise and took our place in the huge queue. Most half decent venues seemed to insist on having queues outside as a sign or suggestion that they were good enough for people to queue outside. Well that might be fine in the summer, no one really minded waiting around talking to people when it was warm. Come winter the whole scenario was just a farce. All of the excuses that it took time to search people and for them to pay in didn't wash. When was the last time that it took two hours for a queue of two thousand fans to get into a football match? Fans had to pay and get searched there as well. No, most clubs did all they could to slow a queue down to the most painful pace possible. It was only places like the Final Frontier where there was a queue at the end of the month purely because they could sell the event three times over and you had to get there at ten to get in. The difference there was that they got the queue moving and they didn't waste time with ridiculous procedures like door pickers. They employed plenty of security staff, allowing more than one person to be searched at once, gave you a thorough check and got you moving. They also had the decency to go to the queue and give people a realistic assessment of their chances of getting in before the place got overcrowded. Not here though, there was a picker, dressed like something off a nineteen seventies David Bowie LP cover, hovering around telling the bouncers who he didn't want at his club. The style Police were well and truly in operation tonight. Jeff was turned away on the grounds that this ridiculous creature, a ghost from a time when he probably wasn't born had taken a dislike to Jeff's collars. We left with him, there was no way that I was going to go in if that was their attitude. We were reassured further back the line that the real reason we didn't get in was because we were in a three and that they didn't let in groups where there were more boys than girls. So much for the club scene moving into the nineties. We dropped Jeff off at Club UK. Summer and myself went home. I was a bit disillusioned by the clubs elitism, which seemed so far removed from the loving egalitarian atmosphere on the dance floor and positively contrary to dancing on the beach with Steve's crowd.

Can You Feel It

The next evening I still couldn't build up the energy or appetite for clubbing and the cinema was Summers' idea. I hadn't been in ages but in a way it was quite a pleasant change not to be out all weekend. We went to see an English film called the 'Young Poisoner's Handbook.' The central character in the film had a chemistry set, hidden in the garden shed which he used to wipe out the rest of his family. The idea of playing around with chemicals was uncannily familiar, it brought back all too clearly the images of our failed attempts to produce ecstasy. Reassuringly he had his methodological problems, suffering at least one large explosion. Chemistry was best kept out of the bedroom I concluded. It was like any business you didn't try to control every link in the production to supply schedule, no it was best to leave that to the experts.

I came out of the film thinking that things had changed a lot since then, there were no high street shops where you could go and just buy a couple of pounds of whatever chemicals you wanted. I remembered getting a junior chemistry set myself and going to the local toy shop where you could get all manner of chemicals to play around with. That just wasn't possible anymore. Not a bad thing I suppose after all if Lewis with a science degree had managed to blow up the flat then heavens knows what the ordinary punter would do.

Summer had enjoyed it. She couldn't get over how unlovable the central character was, she had a point, he'd killed or maimed most of those around him as he bungled his way through life. I wrestled my mind away from ecstasy and started to enjoy her conversation. We walked through the crush of the late evening rush around Leicester Square and Piccadilly towards the relative quietness of Glasshouse Street and the Atlantic Bar and Grill.   Unusually there wasn't a queue and we were quickly ushered in by a tall elegant African girl, with long straightened hair which framed her strong classical features. It was the first time that I'd taken Summer there and she enthusiastically soaked up the atmosphere and the well worn glamour of the art deco interior.

She said that she'd really been looking forward to last night and it was a real pity that we couldn't get in. We sat and finished the evening off in the bar and went back to my flat.

It was late on Sunday morning before I woke. Shit, I'd been supposed to play football, somehow I'd always been able to make it even if I'd been to an all nighter. They'd have already kicked off by now. My head was banging like a eurobeat kick drum. It was first time in weeks that I'd had a few drinks and I'd forgotten to drink gallons of water before going to bed. Summer was still lying there half hidden by the duvet and oblivious to my peril. I eventually dragged myself from the bed and coaxed out Summer. I really hadn't been interested in sex since I'd been doing the pills. This morning I was grateful for the absence of the E related lethargy and I felt that I really should be doing something.

I might have missed football but there was still time to catch the morning Sunday markets. We drove the short distance to the East End, parked up on the Roman Road and went for something to eat, my weekend appetite was back with a vengeance. Breakfast was orange juice steaming hot, home made hot chocolate and croissants. We sat eating them in a converted stable just off the main drag of Colombia Row, just by one of the pubs that the Krays used to frequent. The cool chill of the outbuilding was a welcome refrain from the heat and the hustle bustle of Colombia Row. The market itself was busier than The Final Frontier at the end of the month. We walked and marvelled at the myriad types of cheap and exotic plants and flowers. I bought Summer a bunch of wild, mixed, long stemmed flowers and settled for a pair of trained potted purple cabbages. There was something English about them, rather like those ornamental stone pineapples that adorned the walls of country estates. We gave up on the idea of going down to the shambles of Brick Lane Market which normally resembles the worlds largest flea market on a Sunday morning. Summer was keen to go up to Camden rather than going straight home.

There were Police every where as we drove along the ring road past Angel tube. It was obvious that something big was going on. It all clicked, as I remembered that one of the underground party 'phone lines had been giving out information about a reclaim the streets demonstration. I wasn't sure whether it would be my type of thing, I had a car which I used a lot and the main attraction of the alternative life style that I was getting an insight into revolved around pills and music and to be honest it wasn't worth going to it unless there was a chance to have a dance, there were too many other things going on. Besides whilst most clubbers are eco friendly they all use cars to go raving in. The original raves wouldn't have been possible without the car. Mixmag pointed this out in their history of the rave joking that the invention of the car was an important date in the history of house music. I claimed a parking place just South of the Angel and only just outside the area which was being 'reclaimed'. Summer looked bewildered and didn't seem to be too happy at what was happening around us.

"Don't worry we're just going to have a look, its a peaceful protest and the Police can't touch us if we don't do anything wrong." I reassured her. I loved her dearly but, I could never reconcile her verve for the unusual which was so often contradicted by an irrational fear of the unthreatening unknown.

The Police presence appeared to be overwhelming in terms of numbers but they weren't able to do anything about the twenty foot high pieces of scaffolding tubing which were erected like clothless tepees outside the tube station effectively blocking off the entire street. At the apex of these contraptions protesters were hauled up by simple block and tackle, sitting in slings, surveying the reclamation below them , knowing that the Police were powerless to move them for fear of precipitating injury or worse. We walked past these contraptions and as we got through the initial group of party goers we saw a battalion of walkers emerge from Liverpool Road on our left. This entirely peaceful protest was led by a personal carrier, painted in camouflage greens and greys and bedecked with triumphant revellers dressed in luminous green, orange and yellow workmen's waistcoats, their faces covered by anti radiation masks reminiscent of the earlier days of rave.

Can You Feel It

They stopped in the middle of the six lanes of Upper Street, normally one of the busiest roads in London. The troops opened up what I took to be doors at the back of the small tank to reveal huge bullet shaped loud speakers, which immediately began to emit ear piercing hard-core, gabber and rave music, which was occasionally interrupted by snatches of sober spiel from Melody FM. radio. The crowd loved it, going wild in the strong midday sunshine. I wanted to get straight into it and join the wide eyed boys and girls but for one thing the music wasn't exactly what I was dancing to at The Final Frontier and I was aware that Summer was a little uncertain of the whole situation. The novelty seemed to appeal, but she told me that she was rather wary of the great unwashed masses with their tattoos. She wasn't used to seeing white men with dreadlocks grungey clothes and their unhealthy looking dogs. I tried to explain that its who you are and not what you look like that matters.

We walked around the site taking in all around us. There were two other focal points for dancing, a bus shelter provided a stage for an indie type rock band. The other dance area hadn't really got going, someone had rather enthusiastically wires up a Sinclair C5 electric mini car to a cassette deck, amplifier and speakers. The gremlins seemed to have got the better of it. Summer found this particularly amusing. We both laughed admiringly at the ingenuity of the people who had dumped several tons of sand on the road to provide a play pit for families. There were happy, smiling children playing with buckets and spades in the middle of Upper

Can You Feel It

Street, central London. It was their ebullient glee at the escape from the restraints of urban life that epitomised the rational of the afternoon. We moved on and found ourselves seats on a wall, soaked up the atmosphere and basked in the revitalising sun.

There we were participating in probably in the largest unlicensed outdoor rave in London so far this summer. The Criminal Justice Act had proved powerless to stop the dedicated few from enjoying themselves and conjuring up the real spirit of community and unity that is celebrated in the human desire to party and dance. I thought about getting some E, Summer wanted some beer but I abstained worried about driving home and besides I always fell asleep drinking in the afternoon.

Passers by joined in as did bus drivers and their passengers. We danced with a thin elderly suited Asian man with a can of tennants in his hands and an incredulous smile on his face.

"Got any Khat, my friend?" he kept asking me, I just laughed, I think he must have thought that I was Morrisey with a bunch of flowers or khat as the case maybe just ready to take out of my back pocket. The police stood and watched on one side of the road a film crew took the high ground on the top of a office block. As if not to be out done party-goers scaled the building opposite. Precariously swinging on scaffold and dancing on the parapets as they reached the top. I hoped that it was only the adrenaline that was keeping them going, not wanting the afternoon ruined by the next days probable headlines about 'boys who thought they could fly' or worse. Thankfully it all passed without out incident apart from a bit of a disagreement between Police and reticent hangers on who refused to disperse after the organisers declared the party over.

The fire-brigade arrived to shut off hydrant which had been opened to provide a twenty foot high jet of water to cool thirsty and sweaty party-goers. They left to the sound of not too unfriendly barracking and reasonable cries for the hydrant to be left on to alleviate the effects of the stifling afternoon sun. A couple of young boys grappled bare hands against the large brass washer that had only moments earlier been firmly secured. Their wet, red hands contorted as did their facial expressions, bravely attempting the impossible. We sat and chilled talking about music and clubbing. People came and went and there was a general air of relaxation, friendliness a sense of community and purpose. It was the same coherence which had threaded itself through this remarkable summer.

Summer started clubbing in a big way and she totally out did me on the scene. She had the energy to party night in and night out, emerging only just long enough to see me occasionally before she took another breath of air and dived into the deep underground scene We stayed together through all of this and there was no hint that she might have wanted to go off with anyone else, I was happy on that front. I was worried a bit about the type of people that she started to hang around with. There were stories of going to S&M clubs which certainly weren't all about posing and being seen to be on the scene. These were the hard and rough establishments were you only went if you wanted to take part in what was supposed to go on. They seemed to be beyond the remit of the scene that was welcoming me with open arms. Whilst I was wary of this I was just as quick not to be too judgmental. I might have introduced her to clubbing but if she wanted to go her own way, that was her decision.

She met all manner of diverse people at these events and most of them seemed to have relatively sad existence's which they tried to forget in their nights of escapism. Summer didn't really need that. When we went out it was a different type of escapism, a celebration of life and the appreciation of all that we enjoyed. She made friends with a chap called Ronny who ran a Smarts Drink Stall at Techno City. That had its advantages, we could get in on the guest list, honour of honours and also she could be with me when I was with the boys but could retire to behind the Smart Drinks bar or up to the VIP area as Ronny's guest and chill and meet those all important DJs. I joined her up there on a few occasions but I didn't want to shatter too many illusions by meeting my favourite DJs and finding out that they were just normal people.

One night I'd just dropped off Summer at The Techno City. It must have been about ten o'clock because she was helping out Ronny that night. I came out of the building and jumped down the stairs as I was in a hurry to get back home and to get ready to go somewhere else. There was only one person waiting outside. A young lad of about eighteen, with long dark hair and a harrington jacket. I made friendly conversation saying that he was there early and that I wouldn't be getting back there until about two or three in the morning.

Can You Feel It

With that he was convinced that I must be a DJ. I had to disabuse him of the idea but I must say that it was rather flattering to have someone think that you were one of this generations demigods.

Leo Price rang again, he was full of how he'd hobbled out for his village rugby team to make up the numbers in a local derby match. I told him that at his age that he shouldn't be doing things like that. He wanted to know what my news was.

I had loads of news but most of it would only get him over concerned. "No news."

"Come on, I can tell that something is wrong. Listen, I'm getting a bit worried about you, you might not be flat on a slab yet but you want to be able to reach my age and still play a bit of rugger or football, don't you? I've known people with skag habits that would make you look like the proverbial choir boy slipping out for a quick fag behind the bike sheds. You might say that you're in control but I can tell that you're tired. E might not be the monster that the press make it out to be but you can still totally lose it on E."

He was right I suppose but I didn't feel like there was a problem, I was having the time of my life and I didn't need looking after. I told him that there was someone on the other line and that I'd get back to him. Perhaps I should have just suggested that we both had a night on the E together but I knew that he wouldn't be up for that. It was a friendship that worked best over the telephone and there was no point boring each other, with one of us having to act like a fish out of water.

Can You Feel It

James and Lewis had gone to Ibiza after all. They had both needed the break after the stress of the disaster at my flat. At least James was back on speaking terms and after a couple of weeks at the top clubs in the worlds wildest resort he was a lot more receptive to the idea of going ahead with organising a club night than I'd expected. James was eager to tell me about the girl that he'd met on holiday but was talked down by Lewis who was pleased to say that she had compared him unfavourably with her ex boyfriend who she called handbrake. James felt positively small, inadequate and distinctively humiliated at her description and as well as trying to recover his lost pride he was desperate that we didn't tell Claire anything about it. At least he could count on us for that, we'd all been through quite alot together and we were out to give him a barracking not a real hard time.

Surprisingly Lewis had to drop out of the plans for the club, his ex wife had done the dirty on him allowing the Building Society to repossess their house at a fraction of what they'd paid for it. He had to find huge amounts of money and despite the returns that we were hoping to make on the party he couldn't commit the time favouring round after round of meetings with his lawyers and advisers in an attempt to stave off bankruptcy. If we made a mint then we could always give him the cash. Lewis regarded it all as a bit of a joke, nothing really seemed to penetrate that cool exterior and if it did he certainly wasn't going to tell the world about it.

Underground Resistance

For some strange reason all of London's harder clubs played on a Friday leaving just a few smaller non central clubs to cater for Saturday night Techno. Glamorous commercial house was de rigour on Saturday. There's always an exception to the rule and I first became aware of it idly browsing through the pages of Time Out one Wednesday lunch time.

A massive party was going to be held at a set of railway arches near Tower Bridge. Jeff Mills and Ritchie Hawtin were the big attractions but I made the fatal mistake of leaving tickets until Saturday. That was a bit like trying to buy your Cup Final tickets on the day.

Fat Cat had sold out, Zoom were engaged and the event's own telephone booking system had stopped taking messages. With a mixture of desperation and anticipation Jeff, James and I headed down early nine thirty for a ten thirty start. The place was road blocked hours before it opened. The news on the grapevine was that if we didn't have tickets or reservations three am would be the earliest that we could enter the hallowed arches.

The vibe was amazing. It was the first onet for months, they'd had venue problems so it was going to be a really big one and probably the first time most people had heard Jeff Mills since the Tribal Gathering. We needed no encouragement to stay in the queue.

Underground Resistance

Everyone was chatting and the word was there were two queues one for tickets and the other one for telephone reservations. We'd have to pitch in the latter and try and bluff our way in. I remembered the number I'd rung and when the doorman came down the queue asking, name and how many we said "Green, three."

"There's no Green, on here. When did you ring?

"Today at about three thirty." I tried it on.

"It was all booked up by then." Came the firm reply.

"Well the girl certainly took my booking, if it helps I can remember your number." I stretched my luck.

I recited the number to him. I had rung it but far too late to be booked on the list

He didn't give us the crucial entry passes but then again he didn't turn us away as he'd done with the streams of other hopefuls.

"Wait there, I'll see what I can do." he said working his way down the queue. We stood back at the gate as others filed through. We talked to most of those going in. Before the doorman got back we'd been offered free passes from a large group from Portsmouth Not all of them had turned up and not all of them might make it. There was a tremendous surge of adrenaline as we passed through the gates and the obligatory search.

The underpants were the last refuge of the Ecstasy tablet. No one ever checked there. Some clubs even checked girls bras and asked for shoes and socks to be taken off. I emptied my pockets on the table and was thoroughly searched from head to toe. It was with enormous relief that my tablets remained undetected. I'd rather smuggle them in than take them in the queue outside. I preferred to get there early, sit and chat and gradually come up at leisure.

When inside after walking through the interlinked railway arches. We decided to sit out in the warm moonlit night. A white boy with travellers locks tried to swap his weed for hash. He offered me an E for ten quid after previously telling me what E's he rated and he didn't rate the one he was selling. He'd described it as crap but now it was a really good pill. He harmlessly and persistently put his case but found no takers. It was good rib tickling entertainment. He moved on elsewhere.

It was a blistering summer and this probably the warmest night so far. The stars were actually visible over Tower Bridge. Inside the arches filled up and we rapidly perspired to the energetic jazzy funky beat. Derek May was right when he described techno as what you would have got if George Clinton and Kraftwerk were stuck in a lift with a synthesiser. This was techno played at its best. Even my shoes were soaking when I went out to chill and my heart was beating faster than the music. I was catching rather than taking breaths, someone put their hand on my knee and grinned, sitting with me for a while. Everytime I went back in I couldn't last for more than twenty minutes. The music was brilliant but physically I couldn't cope. I was E-d up but not E'd up so much that I didn't know what was going on.

After I 'd been in and out three or four times I realised that James and Greg were still in there. It took a lot of persuasion to get them outside but I think they realised why I'd dragged them out. We sat and talked to a group of real people we had met pushing into to the queue at the Final Frontier. It was great to see them again, we saw them at most of the big hard house and techno events, it was refreshing to see that all the pleasantries which people exchange at these parties aren't just shallow and meaningless. There were lots of deep and lasting friendships forged out there as a result of dance music. To a lot of people the weekend high is the most important thing in their lives, and why not?

James spent the rest of the evening sleeping in the chill out room, just how he managed it, wet through and loved up, I don't know.

It was over before it started and come six o'clock we made our weary way to the car, agreeing that it was one of the best nights in a long time. We were besieged by the usual crowd of early morning flyer brigade.

" Now, now, now, what have you been up to?" laughed one of the flyer girls in the direction of Jeff, as he stood there totally bedraggled. We all smiled, she had a point, he was soaked to the skin, absolutely dripping.

We nearly emptied a crate of coke that I had in the boot of the car. Some people won't touch fizzy drinks on E but this went down a real treat. We all decided that if we were going to put a night on of our own then we'd have to do it along these lines, that there too many house nights and that there was a gap in the market for a Saturday night techno night.

James came back to mine and we spent most of Sunday morning planning what we were going to do. The bus garage that I'd seen previously was being squatted as a car park but at least the local paper were on their case. I'd make enquires as to what the state of play was. I knew that it had been bought by Super Foods for store development. Certainly the supermarket wasn't going to allow that to go on for much longer.

Jeff reluctantly had to drop out. He was really keen on the idea but often didn't leave the office until eleven at night and doubted whether he could really help to make a valuable contribution, with the preparation and logistical planning of the event. He was as big a techno fan as me and while I wanted him on board there was just no way that he could juggle his responsibilities like James and myself. He was even finding it difficult to find time to see a really cute young girl that he'd met at the Ministry.

So we were back to where we were just before my flat had witnessed Lewis' spectacular pyrotechnics, we knew exactly what we wanted to do it was just a matter of putting the bits together. I didn't for one minute think that it was going to be easy but at least we had a well thought out business plan. We decided to call it 'Well Mobbed', we didn't want a glitzy or futuristic name, all that had been done before, we just wanted the name to be a self fulfilling prophecy. We were going to make a huge success of it, there was no mistaking that.

I'd also thought about insurance and how we'd guarantee that the night went well. What I mean is that I was going to control the pills for the night. James wasn't going to know, he'd be a liability on that front and anyway if I got Steve involved there'd be no need for James to do anything. The pills would help on two fronts, if we didn't sell enough tickets to break even then at least we'd have a reserve fund to balance the books and of course an E'd up crowd is a happy crowd. It had to be done and I knew where the pills were coming from.

Work was a struggle as I tried to do two jobs at once, it was hard enough to keep pace with what I was paid to do never mind ringing a hundred and one different people to get the best quotes for everything we needed.

Leo Price was a welcome respite.

"Hello dear boy, so what have you been up to this weekend, anymore wild adventures, torrid tales or grave causes for concern?"

His animated, erudite tones brought a smile to my face, lifting me out of what for all intents and purposes had been a deep psychological torpor. I'd been day dreaming and I couldn't see out of the dark amorphous room that was Tuesday morning.

"Well you probably won't wont to hear this but you're going to."

"Hear what, come on now spill it all out, haven't got all day," he chuckled, "lets have the news."

I told him that we'd had a mega weekend and that I was going to promote a big club night. I might as well have told him that I was going to take control of the Colombian cocaine trade.

"Oh my god, No you're not serious are you. You'll have to be careful you know, this is all getting a bit out of hand, what would work say if you were becoming a major player in what for all intents and purpose is the drugs world."

He'd go bananas if I told him exactly what was going to go on.

Underground Resistance

"It's okay," I said, "sounds worse than it is, should be a really good laugh and a chance to make a bit of pocket money. Besides things like this should open a few doors and guest lists if you know what I mean.

He wasn't interested how this was going to effect me socially, he had my professional interests at heart.

"Listen old boy, its about time that we had a serious sit down chat and took you through all of this head to head. It might be a laugh now but think of your job, they don't know do they? What happens if it all goes up in flames, where are you then, it's not as if you could ever work again. The Institute would see to that, I suggest Quaglingos tomorrow at eight thirty."

"I can't." I couldn't, it would just make matters worse. I felt in control to an extent. I valued his help on the 'phone but I couldn't think of a worse way to spend the evening talking about somebody else's concerns. I had it all covered and I didn't need confusing at this stage.

"Oh, well suit yourself, offer rejected, offer retracted, I would have paid you know."

"Thanks, it's just something that I think that I can keep a lid on, to me it's as good as admitting defeat if I start to blab out exactly what I feel."

"Oh, well play it your own way but make sure that you keep in touch. I might not be your man if you need a ton of E but I'm always here if you want a quick chat in confidence."

I knew that I could trust him with just about anything and I valued his good Samaritan calls. We used to just chat and share gossip on a quid pro quo basis, now I was doing all of the taking and none of the giving. It was a reminder that everything was getting out of kilter, he was right I had to do something before it all blew up in my face.

I really enjoyed all the partying and the Es but on days like this I felt that I was in a bad film and that the plot was coming to an end. There wasn't enough time to rewrite it. The credits were about to roll and I wanted to be watching and not starring in it.

I checked the venue after work and the squatters had gone I'd ring the owners and suggest that they got some reputable clients for at least one Saturday night of the month.

There was some one else that I had to ring, I hadn't seen Dick since Wimbledon but he was my first and best line of enquiry when it came to stocking up with a few pills.

I couldn't tell Summer about this, she'd go absolutely mad and whilst I thought she was really brilliant I just didn't know how much I could trust her. Anyway from when I first spoke to Dick it was fairly obvious that she wasn't privy to any of his drug related business and I couldn't risk rubbing up him the wrong way.

Summer and I was to a really mad night at one of the smarter central London house parties. There were models and personalities everywhere. She loved the glamorous atmosphere, soaking up all the attention which she received. Her bubbly personality, gregarious nature, wonder bra tops and attractive features meant that she was seldom out of the spotlight. Normally I didn't mind who she spoke to or what she did but when some guy, monopolised her for a while I was a bit concerned. I'd seen him before and I think I remembered Steve saying that he was called Marc Campbell, leader of a south London gang and heavily involved in drugs. He looked it in an obvious manner, which was odd in two ways, first of all we were at an upmarket club, I'd never seen a dealer in there and it was the type of place that actually registered good alcohol sales compared with a lot of club land. Not the type of place that would entertain two bit villains. Secondly I'd heard that gangsters today didn't want to draw attention to their activities and that they dressed and acted like normal members of society. Not this guy, if he was who I thought he was then he was doing it all by the old school methods. Rather like a football fan who hasn't heard of 'soccer casuals' fifteen years on and thinks that Dr Marten boots and drain pipe trousers are where it's at. Summer told me not to worry and that he'd just been talking about this and that but as I said there was something not quite right about it.

Mantra to the Buddha

I knew that if I was going to buy pills and a lot of pills at discount prices that I'd have to do it from someone that I knew and thought that I could trust. Well in reality that meant Dick, Steve couldn't deliver in those quantities and buying on from a dealer in England who'd probably got pills which came from Holland in the first place meant that the price wouldn't be competitive. Well, when I say trust when it came to Dick I hardly knew him, I didn't really know if I could trust him but here I was asking him to put me in touch with his supplier in the Netherlands. My words came out quietly and slowly they were almost drowned by the mix tape playing in the latest Westbourne Grove designer bar.

"Jerry," he said, looking concerned, "There are many things I can tell you. You have first to convince me that you will not tell things to others and that you can pull this off without drawing attention to yourself or others."

"Don't worry," I said, "I've got it all planned out, every aspect's covered. I am going to France on a one day special offer, you know the type that they advertise in the papers, a pound a person and a tenner for the car. I'll be a shopper for all intents and purpose, except I'll be going a little further than the average day tripper and I'll be bringing back a little more than wine, beer and cheese. Once I'm in Holland I'll leave my car in the centre of the local town, walk or get a taxi to the pick up point and make sure that I'm not followed on the way back to the

163

Mantra To The Buddha

car. Back in Calais I'll load up with the normal type of cargo and no one will be the wiser. As for the pills themselves I thought about putting them in a spare tyre but I read about someone getting caught doing that recently. No, the rear bumper on some Jaguars are only held on by one bolt. I know I've had mine stolen before. I was going to get around to having it welded on but before I do that I'll bring back the goods inside it. They'll be wrapped so that the dogs cannot smell them and the beauty of the bumper is that they can't prove that it was you who put the drugs there, it could have been anyone with ten minutes access to the car in Holland, someone who knew I was going abroad and took advantage of the fact. I thought about doing it to someone myself but this time I decided that I'd be best being in control. I wouldn't be able to handle anyone else being stopped for my pills. I'm not that ruthless yet. If they catch me what have they got? An accountant of twenty-nine years of age, previous good character. If it had to go before a jury I'd be happy to take my chances."

"Well thought out I am impressed but what about the money I don't want to hear that there have been huge cash transactions, you know that the banks have to report those don't you?"

"Yeah, it's my business to know that. I've withdrawn cash over the last couple of weeks, nothing too big or out of the ordinary. Then there's a couple of grand I am borrowing supposedly to buy a painting. I am actually buying the painting but not with cash but my friend doesn't know that, if anything he thinks that I am doing him a favour by looking after a bit of loose cash that the tax man doesn't need to know about.

"Very good but how do you think that you'll cope at customs?"

"Well I'd hope not to get stopped but I 'm sure that I could be cool and natural enough. I get a lot of practice at work in dealing in difficult situations, I'm not suggesting that I have to do anything like this but you know its not as if I'll be starting off completely green."

"Well, you must not tell anyone and I mean anyone that this is happening. I'll write you out the address and telephone number you're not to use it until you get to the Netherlands. I'll put you in touch and arrange a meeting time. As soon as you've done the deal you're to get rid of the details. There must be nothing to link you to them if you get stopped."

"It will be on a Saturday at 13:00. Five minutes late and it's all off. They've got what you want and at the price we talked about. Do not change your money to Guilders that will be suspicious. Do not hide it in the car when you go over that will be suspicious if it is found hidden. The English Police could confiscate it if they were able to satisfy a court that it could be drugs related"

He took a sip of his designer beer bottle and left. It was all up to me now.

I gave Steve a ring, I hadn't spoken to him for a while. I'd been too wound up in what was going on around me. He did all of the talking, he was having a hard time of it what with Jules leaving him and all of the hassle from the Police I wasn't able to entice him out to get things off his mind. Someone had rung him up again   repeating   the

Mantra To The Buddha

threat that the next time that he worked his pitch there'd be a knife waiting for him. It was as if he just had to tell me about it he didn't want advice or to talk about it so we dropped the subject. I told him about that brilliant night house night that I'd been to with Summer. I was spending a lot of time with her now. Of course I got ribbing off the boys about that but it didn't stop me going out, if anything I was out and about more than them. I described the crowd that they got there, the more up for it dressed up model, the avant garde as they boasted on the door and the occasional face that stood out in the crowd. He confirmed that the big South American I'd seen speaking to Summer was Marc Campbell. Steve said that Campbell was ruthless, part of a south London gang that knew no rules or boundaries. He was bad news and Steve said that we should have avoid him at all costs. Steve said that he owned quite a few of the dance clubs and restaurants but that he was surprised that the likes of Campbell were allowed within shooting distance of where we'd seen him.

Summer and I went back to the same club the next week, luckily there was no Campbell this time, he cannot have got past the door. It must have just been our bad luck to run into him last time. Paul Oakenfold was delayed in Sweden or somewhere but the resident DJ kept everyone rocking all night long. We got a minicab home, the African driver was more fun than the car which creaked every time we went round a corner. We'd only got as far as Kings Cross when we were pulled by the Police. Apparently we'd been doing sixty in a thirty and they wanted to check his hire and reward mini cabbing

Mantra To The Buddha

insurance. He'd obviously been here before and asked us to call him Ken and say that we were just friends. Well I'm not sure what it was, whether it was the persistence of the Police or the fact that ecstasy makes it really hard to tell anything other than the truth but our man was in trouble. So was I come to that, I had two pills in my socks and I was sure that I was going to get searched. My pupils were like king sized pizzas and it must have been obvious that I was doved up.

The Police asked us for our names and addresses and we obliged, they wanted to know why we had blue bottles with us but were happy with my reply that they were just bottles of mineral water. That was the truth so there was no problem there and either the Police didn't put two and two together or they thought that they needed us to make out a case against our minicab driver.

It was only when I got home and took my shoes off that I realised that I was in big trouble. I couldn't find the pills anywhere. I must have dropped them in the cab when I was panicking. The Police had my name and address and the pills were in a plastic bag, that would have my prints on it. There was nothing to but sit back and wait for a telephone call or a knock on the door

Summer was oblivious to all of this, she'd had a real trippy E and wasn't able to understand what was going on at the road side never mind give the officers a coherent response. Luckily I'd done all of the talking for her. I tried to explain my predicament to her but the message didn't get through. I paced around the flat and eventually followed her into the bedroom where she was crouched down on her knees, face to the mattress and almost

167

completely covered by the duvet. Amused at her strange position I asked what she was doing.

"Watching the bunnies, I think I'd like to play with them now," she said obviously totally out of it and really enjoying herself.

That cheered me up a bit and so as to forget the inevitable I decided that she needed some company in bed, she could play with me as well as her bunnies. It was only when I took my underpants off that I realised that it was all going to be all right. The pills were there, I hadn't lost them after all I'd taken them out of my shoes as the Police were stopping us and forgotten all about it. I'd have to be a lot more careful from now remembering that most of the arrests I'd heard of were of people coming out of rather than going into clubs. I suppose that even the Police had sussed that your guard's going to be a lot lower after a night on the E.

Acperience

Nobody else had turned up at the pub. It was just Graham and I. We sat outside the pub amongst the midweek early evening drinkers, a mixture of office workers and those more comfortably attired. Graham quietly began to tell me the effects of the E that he'd taken the night before the Oxford party. I sat in shock and bewilderment. It must have been months ago and still he got panic attacks. They plagued him at the most inopportune moments. Today had been a milestone, the first time that he'd found the courage to use the tube. Previously he'd been racked with fear at the mere thought. Every time he heard music with a solid four-four beat, the association was enough to get him worried, he thought that he was only sixty per cent psychologically recovered from his experience.

He'd been to his doctor. It had taken him ages to do that, he wasn't sure how it would look a man in his position, whether the Doctor would respect his wish for privacy, whether his wife or employer would find out. As it turned out there was little chance of the Doctor talking to anyone about it. He dismissed Graham worries saying that they were self inflicted and that a man of his age and standing should be able to pull himself out of the mess he'd got himself into. Fat lot of use that was.

His wife, he couldn't really tell her, she came from a normal stable background and the longer he left it the harder it got. He was convinced that it could only add to his problems if she found out about it.

169

Acperience

There were days when he thought that he couldn't cope with the simplest tasks. He felt like his entire world was caving in. He got round to preparing a resignation letter on several occasions. Each time though he managed to find an extra reserve of resolve to convince himself that it would all be over soon.

He didn't seem to blame me or anyone else, it had been his decision. James probably hadn't helped by ringing him up half a dozen times before we went out on the evening in question. James had joked that it was only five hours before he died of his first E. The next call was half an hour later and on the lines that Graham would be dead in four and a half hours. Not really the best way to prepare a good friend for his first experience on E. Whilst that probably didn't help the likely cause of the problem was something to do with Graham's level of Monoanine Oxidiase being incompatible with the pure Methleydioxymethampethamine and that it had caused depression rather than elation. Not everyone's physiological make up is the same and of course as in everything there has to be the exception to the rule. It was just Grahams bad luck to find that out by mistake.

I can remember vividly being told at the club that Graham was having problems and that he needed somebody to sit with him. I recall taking over shifts from James and Greg.

Graham had been a picture of anguished resolve. Like a man with a red hot poker pressed to his naked flesh, stifling his screams by biting on a leather bit.

Acperience

He held my hand crushing my fingers as every wave of anxiety surged through him. His other hand pushed down clenching his open fist into the flesh of my thigh.

Remarkably he had lasted the duration that evening. He reminded me that we had all left together at six am and gone back to my house. He was adamant that he would have gone home earlier but was glued to his seat, he couldn't move or contemplate going anywhere. Never mind by himself.

There was no doubt that just one tablet had caused such damaging effects. It was a tablet from the same batch that the rest of us had had a good night on. Graham had taken the precaution of having a half first, waiting for over half an hour and had only felt the full effects after taking the full tablet.

Graham said that he was never ever going to even think about taking drugs again, it was obvious that they didn't work for him and he went as far to say that at one stage he seriously had thought that he was looking at a life in an institution, purely because he'd lost his self resolve. The only positive factor he saw in the whole scenario was that his views towards those less able in society had become a lot less critical. It had given him insight to the fact that whilst we might live in a so called egalitarian society that a lot of people were handicapped by a lot more than laziness in life's struggle.

I was over the ecstasy honeymoon period. I wasn't still in love but it wasn't a relationship that had run its natural course. E and I still had good times together. Graham's experience was a disturbing one but it was Graham's experience. I had no real problems and I didn't envisage them. I might get the blues occasionally but I was not going to dance myself to death

I got the impression that whilst Graham didn't disapprove of his friends doing one he would have been happier if we had all grown out of it by now.

I tried to cheer him up by telling a theory that I'd developed that day. It was suggested in the newspapers that Sir Isaac Newton was an alchemist and had been heavily involved in the occult using nutmeg amongst other essential oils to reach a higher state of consciousness. It was suggested that it was only by reaching these states that he was able to formulate his scientific theories of gravity. Nutmeg of course is widely known as a kitchen narcotic and contains amongst essential oils, elemicin and myristicin which when mixed with the ammonia that naturally occurs in vitro in the liver produce a chemical remarkably similar to ecstasy in composition and effect. I joked to Graham that rather than watching an apple descend, Newton's law owed more to him becoming aware that, 'he who gets high must also come down.' Graham managed a laugh of sorts, adding that it had been his own bad luck not to have experienced the high part of the equation.

When I got home there was a message on the answer machine from someone who obviously hadn't grown out of E. It was Tony, he'd finally managed to drag himself away from a series of beach parties that had pretty much mapped out the Pacific rim. He was on his way home and from what he said it looked like he was going to be back in time for our party. He was going to be pretty amazed at the extent that I'd got into the scene in just a few long summer months.

Summer was keen to meet Tony, she got on with most of my friends but was intrigued to meet the man who'd introduced me to E. We sat and watched a TV documentary about the use of Ecstasy and the research that had gone into it. I'd seen it before but it was Summer who yelled, "there's Jeremy Healy!" when they showed a few brief clips of a party in an aircraft hanger in Lydd, Kent. Maybe it was him but I didn't recognise him. Summer was getting into this in a big way she'd started to buy heaps of records and was in danger of becoming a bit of a trainspotter. Still at least she wasn't waking me up at three in the morning to tell me which records she'd like to mix or buy. Hers was a healthy interest, so perhaps it was a bit unfair to call her a trainspotter. Trainspotters were generally regarded as the type of person who went to a night club and instead of treating it just like a fun night out, turned it into an exercise in trying to master advanced engineering by watching all that a DJ did and prided themselves in knowing which mix of which record was playing, who had produced it and which label it was on. It was an obsessive interest which bordered on the eponymous nick name it had been rightly given. It had nothing to do with the repetitive and compulsive behaviour which the programme attributed to the use of E, it was just an overactive interest in what was spinning on the wheels of steel.

We were both undeterred by the programmes analysis of animal research which showed that large areas of the brain were destroyed with constant Ecstasy use. After the

Acperience

programme was first shown, these results were put into context when it was highlighted that the amount of Ecstasy which had caused the problems with the mice was the equivalent to me drinking a bath full of whisky. No despite Grahams problems and the stories I read in the press of the occasional apparently Ecstasy related, sad fatality I was more and more convinced that all of this could only do me long term harm if a huge sack of tablets was dropped on me from a great height.

Access

Access

A thin grey early morning mist shrouded the tranquil Kent fields as I sped my way to Dover. I'd stayed at home the night before, Summer had gone away for the weekend with some friends. I was off to visit relatives as far as anyone else was concerned, only myself and Dicks friend in Holland knew that I was really going to spend the rest of this beautiful day drug smuggling. I gazed curiously at the gentle calm of the countryside. Farms and oast houses conjured up images of benign security.

I hadn't really slept and it was a pure adrenaline rush that helped me roar down the empty motorway. This time it had to go to plan, there'd be no explosions, no ill fitting joints and no need to go leaping over balcony rails. All I had to do was to keep cool. I compared it with doing a professional days work, or perhaps just going to the shops to buy something. The stakes were higher and it was absolutely crucial that nothing went wrong, there was no way that I'd cope for fifteen minutes never mind fifteen years in a squalid cell.

I'd had to make sacrifices and that was even more of an incentive. I'd had to stay in on a Friday night, missed the Final Frontier and my body wasn't really sure as to what was going on. Here I was, I'd been up nearly all night, I'd got an adrenaline rush but there wasn't a club in sight. I hadn't had any pills and my body couldn't work out whether it was time to go out or it was time for bed. I was certain that I must have really missed a good night out somewhere but I convinced myself that it didn't matter, these places weren't going to go away in a hurry and by the time that I'd got back tonight then I'd have a guaranteed passport to all night enjoyment.

I relaxed, reclining on the ferries leatherette settee. The polymer reflected my body heat causing a nauseous sweat. I shuffled uncomfortably, wanting to be back in bed but gave up the idea of sleep, deciding that even if I managed some on the boat that I'd probably feel even worse. I went for a walk watching the scrums in the duty free shop.

Holland was wide awake when I got there but as I drove slowly down the narrow shaded street there was that same sense of calm that I'd felt in Kent. The houses were terraced, rendered in plaster with closed shutters. A group of children were playing around the only other car in the street. They paused as I drove by and I was struck by the contrast to London's busy streets where no one stops for anything and parking is at a premium.

Number thirty two was no different to any of the other houses. I drove straight past it and back into the town centre. The town hall clock had just chimed for midday. I decided that it was pointless to hire a car or a taxi, both could be traced back to me. I'd walk, it was less likely to draw attention to myself and besides my destination had looked dreary not dangerous.

It was precisely one o'clock local time when I knocked on the door. I'd set my watch on the ferry, there was no way that I was going to be late for this. The door was opened by a large man in his mid twenties, almost six foot five, the first things I noticed about him were his huge shoulders and fop of blonde hair.

He ushered me inside conducting himself in a gentle manner almost incongruous with his size. We walked down a long dark hallway which resonated the refreshing chill of an old building in summer.

Still, without speaking he ushered me into a small back kitchen."

"Please take a seat," were his first friendly matter of fact words.

I actually felt like standing in the pervading cold but followed his suggestion. As a guest I felt obliged and assured by his calming manner. I was glad that it was just the two of us, there was no way that I would have felt confident going to a strange address with £9,000 in my pockets and doing business with someone I didn't know, they could have had guns, anything I didn't know.

"Don't worry," he laughed, probably sensing my trepidation." There are gangsters in Holland, just like there are in England, we don't have anything to with them."

"Have you got the money," he asked.

I nodded and patted the slight bulge coming from the inside pocket of my leather jacket.

"Not just yet," he said, "let me tell you what we do here. We try to be, I think like English Gentlemen, if you say it like that, here we have a problem with ecstasy, the problem is that we can't make enough of it. There are two types of factories, those like ours which is set up to help people enjoy themselves, we'd be doing something else if Merck still had the patent on the drug and were able to legally distribute it. The other type of factory is run by gangsters who don't care what they put out on to the streets, they sell under strength pills because they know that they can get away with it. Worse than that, if a batch goes wrong or if they haven't made enough for whatever reason, too much Police attention or a lack of materials they just sell any rubbish instead. People say that they send all of the dud pills to England but I don't think so we get a lot of them over here because whilst there are a few outfits that test drugs actually at parties, they're hardly going to be let into a gangster controlled party. We'd like to think that we're completely different to that type of operation. We're a lot smaller of course we make a profit on what we make but so do most businesses, we're not ashamed of that. All we do is to satisfy a need in society, we normally only supply our friends but Dick mentioned you favourably so that's good enough for me.

I listened intentively as he continued, "You will be very careful. In Holland the Police know who we are but they don't give us any trouble, they're not interested, they'd rather catch the other lot, if anyone. The problem would be if the English Police found out about us, then the Dutch Police would be forced to take action to help international relations."

"There's not a chance of me speaking to anyone, anything, no one knows that I've left the country this weekend let alone what I've got up to, and in respect of getting caught Dick probably told you about all the planning that I've put into this."

Access

"Yes, he was very impressed, would you like a biscuit," he said taking the lid off a tin and offering it in my direction.

I said yes out of courtesy, I wasn't really hungry, I smiled as a saw exactly what he was offering me. The tin was full of pills, disco biscuits if you like, hundreds and thousands of them, I'd never seen so many. He smiled and told me that there were exactly three thousand there. He decanted them in to a strong plastic bag and put I the money on the table.

"Don't worry I don't need to count them, " I said, and was surprised to hear him say that he didn't need to count the money. It wasn't exactly how I'd imagined it and I was quite grateful for that. Here we were with three thousand pills and nine thousand pounds in sterling and guilders on the table, like something out of a film and we were just sitting around and chatting as if we'd been discussing football or the weather.

I didn't stay too long, I'd enjoyed our chat and it was good to have company for a while as I'd been on my own since yesterday evening.

Outside I resisted the temptation to run down the dank street fired by the surge of adrenaline that had built up with the excitement of the deal. I walked briskly through the Saturday fruit and vegetable market marvelling at the Mediterranean colours and smells that had somehow found their way so close to the cold, uninviting North Sea.

I'd parked up against a wall, luckily the car park was relatively empty and I don't think that anyone saw me un-bolt the bumper, deposit the pills and wipe everywhere for prints. I drove down the E3 motorway, through Belgium with an enormous feeling of relief and satisfaction. I chuckled to myself thinking that E3 was obviously an anachronism for the three thousand pills that I had with me. The weather was glorious. I turned off the air-conditioning, opened the sunroof all of the windows and the stereo belted out DJ mixtape after mixtape, Danny Rampling, Billy Nasty, Carl Cox and Jeremy Healy all thundered their beats, keeping me awake as I revelled in all that was around me.

I needed to stop soon after Ghent. I hadn't eaten all day and I wasn't going to stay awake if I drove non-stop to Calais. In stark contrast to my normally subdued Saturday appetite I devoured a huge bowl of mussels, chips and French bread. I even managed a couple of slices of latticed French tart with endless cups of coffee.

Back at the car I decided on a ten minute rest. I relaxed in the reclining passengers seat. I woke with a start, never mind ten minutes I'd probably slept for about two hours. I panicked realising that I only had just under two hours to get back to Calais and get the shopping.

I took a few short breaths, slapped my cheeks to make sure that I was fully awake and relaxed, there was no point going on in a panic, that would be worse than actually missing the ferry. I exploited the empty motorway taking full advantage of the Jaguars speed and handling. I'd planned to stop off at the Continental hypermarket in the middle of Calais itself but thought that it would be crammed with Saturday shoppers. Instead I stopped off at the first supermarket I saw. It didn't have a fantastic range of goods but then again all I really needed was beer, wine, cheese and whatever else I could get my hands on. I quickly loaded it up smiling to myself as I recalled the story I'd heard about people actually smuggling pills and the like in beer bottles. At least Customs wouldn't find anything if they looked there.

The traffic was all right as I sped through Calais and I made the ferry with ten minutes to spare. I had time to get out of the car stand and stretch in the sun and even have some of the French bread and cheese that I'd bought. It must have been the nerves that were fuelling my appetite.

Back in Dover no one looked at my passport. I'd switched the mixtapes for Radio Four but there was no one on the Customs channel as I drove through. I accelerated up the long steep hill out of the port only to be confronted by sirens and flashing blue lights. My heart sank but luckily they weren't for me, the Police were pulling over a transit van which was noticeably down on its back wheels, probably beer smugglers I thought.

With that I was convinced that I'd actually done it. I put my foot down again and cruised a neutral eighty five all the way back to London. It was only the Saturday West End bound traffic that slowed me to a crawl.

I made three trips from the car with the shopping each time waiting to see whether the coast was clear so I could remove the bumper. It was literally third time lucky. Back in the flat I opened up the days Times and took out my bag, what should I do? Count them? Taste them or what? I eventually took one out of the bag, it was smaller than I was used to, I measured it as being five millimetres by two millimetres. The rear had a slight graze of a fracture line and the front had what looked like the outline of a crocodile looking rather like the emblem of a well known brand of sports gear. I dabbed it on my tongue, it certainly tasted bitter but I couldn't bring myself to try it not at home by myself.

I'd read a story in the papers about a barrister who'd become overcome by the fumes from a tin of pills which he'd opened as an exhibit before a case was about to start. He had to stop in the middle of his opening speech and tell the judge that he'd done "something silly." He was admitted to hospital with 'classic ecstasy poisoning'. Well here I was with an open bag of three thousand pills, either mine were dud or they were of a dissimilar type to those the barrister sniffed, they certainly didn't smell of anything.

No one else was around, they were either away or were somewhere all ready. I didn't really want to be seen to be around because I wasn't supposed to be in town. I decided on the Ministry, none of my lot would be there, they'd gone off to a party in the country. I had a really good time, despite the fact that I knew no one there I felt as if I had two thousand close mates with me, and I had the reassurance that the pills were really good.

Summer rang in a real flap, Jeremy Healy had died in a car crash. She'd met him not long ago and he'd signed a flyer for her saying, "Summer, you're only as good as your last fucking experience." I did my best to comfort her on the 'phone

I rang James but he just laughed at my sad and sombre announcement. "It was a water sports accident last month, this chap has died more times than he's spun records, just because he's so popular there's a different rumour every week. No, rumours of his death are greatly exaggerated, he'll be playing at Glitteratti on Friday but I must say that it serves him right any one who used to play in a group called Haysi Fantasi deserves to be killed off once in a while."

Not even a dozen 'phone calls to The Cross and Glitterati would change her mind, we had to go up there to see him play, I suppose if all of his fans acted likewise then there was every reason to believe that these rumours started in the Jeremy Healy camp but with such a huge following that probably wouldn't really be necessary. He might not play Detroit Techno all the time but his cueing skills and ear for a good tune meant that his reputation wasn't ill founded.

We were up by The Cross later that weekend at a huge Que Pasa party at Bagley's Warehouse. All the big name DJs were there, it was so packed that it was hard to move. We sat for a breather in what was known as the Powder Room. Summer went off to the ladies and I spoke to a young lad who was on a trip. Suddenly without any warning the lights went up and there were Police all over the place. Summer was just making her way back from the toilets and the lad next to me was cursing the sudden intrusion and shock of the lights. It was probably the E but I needed to speak to the Police and find out what was happening, it was pretty obvious that it wasn't a drugs raid. They weren't really interested in the punters but were asking did anyone see anything?

"See what?" I asked.

"There's been an incident," Replied a senior officer.

Access

Pushing my luck I asked him what type of incident.

"A stabbing," was his terse reply.

Summer and I left, the party was obviously over, I was upset, things weren't meant to happen in clubs like that, it might have been really full but there was no hint of trouble, there never was at this type of place, only people having the time of their lives. When we left we noticed that the Police had taped off about fifteen feet from where I'd been sitting. On the way out of the Goods Yard Summer had to drag me away from the Police officers who I was intent on telling that they were all at the wrong place because there was never any trouble at house parties.

On the news the next day it said that a door steward had been stabbed dead and a colleague was seriously injured. Rumours on the grapevine was that it was a rival security firm trying to muscle in. I found it all quite upsetting, rather like an innocence being shattered, I cheered up a bit when I heard that some one had been arrested, but the bad news clung and exaggerated the weekly come down.

It's Our Future

Its Our Future

I was missing Summer. Sundays desolation dug even deeper tonight. She was away visiting relations. The normal post weekend gloom promised to be lifted when she got back. I remember her saying that she'd ring me. I went to the 'phone several times to ring her but never actually picked up the receiver. It wasn't that I didn't want to swallow my pride and ring her, it was just that I knew if she was back and capable of a coherent conversation then she'd ring me. I don't remember her saying exactly where it was she was going but I got the impression that it was some distance.

She did ring. Late of course and I needed no encouragement to go round at her request. She seemed quite drained and somehow that lifted me. It wouldn't do to have the two of us acting like candidates for a course of prozac. I took the car I'd thought about a taxi but I didn't want to be messing around in the morning. There was nothing worse than having ones fine tuning interfered with at six am.

She literally jumped on me when we came face to face on the door step. She wrapped her arm round my neck and her legs round my waist. We just hugged and kissed like there was no tomorrow. I walked into the lounge still holding her and sat down on the sofa. It really was good to see her.

"So, where've you been," I asked with interest.

"Like I told you, to see some relatives."

185

It's Our Future

"Anywhere groovy?"

"Umm, sort of." She said in a non committal tone. This wasn't the open flowing conversation I'd become used to with her.

"Is there a problem, I am just asking where it was that you, went?"

"Well I've just been away, that's enough isn't it?"

I wasn't sure. I trusted her but I wondered why she was so secretive about it for heavens sake. There was nothing wrong with most of the country, most major centres had a half decent club near them. It didn't matter to me if she'd been to Wolverhampton, Windsor or Washington, Tyne and Wear. I wasn't a geography snob or anything and I just knew that she wasn't having an affair.

I left it and we retired to the bedroom leaving a trail of clothes behind us. I didn't know what was wrong and it really didn't matter, she was back and back with me. I lifted her suitcase off the bed, so as to put it out of the way. She immediately snapped at me grabbing the bag as I started to lift it. It didn't matter. I'd already seen what she wanted to hide. A wad of fifty pound notes, still in a polythene wrap, dropped first onto the edge of the bed and then to the floor.

"Don't worry it's all right," she snapped, "I was going to tell you, I know exactly what I am doing."

"You better had," I said under my breath.

"I've got it all under control."

"I must have lost my temper, I actually shouted at her, " Where the hells all of this come from!"

I listened in astonishment, as she opened up telling me the truth with tears flowing down her cheeks. She held

It's Our Future

herself close to me for comfort and presumably acceptance or forgiveness. She took me back to the night when we'd seen Campbell and his friends. He'd been in touch with her ever since. It was nothing sexual, no it was nothing like that. He'd been testing her out for a position in his organisation. He'd taken her to Cuba for the weekend, left her there while he went on for a weeks business in the States. She'd been left to get on with her own thing, and, oh yes, and he'd asked her to just slip five kilos of cocaine back to Blighty with her. He'd given her a thousand pounds for her services, oh yes and the air fare there and back. I couldn't believe that she'd been so stupid. I realised that she did things on impulsive and lived life for the minute but this didn't exactly fit the bill. This had to have organised way in advance, Campbell can't have held anything over her to make her go and it cannot have been the money. If she'd wanted that she could have asked. I gave up thinking of a motive, that didn't matter, people did stupid things that flew in the face of logic.

I just took it all in and held her closer, telling her that it would be all right. I asked her if she knew that cocaine was worth about sixty quid a gram on the street and that it worked out that she'd only got two hundred a kilo which would probably be cut four or five times before it hit the street. I went through the chances of getting caught at one of the worlds securest airports, she'd flown in through Heathrow for heavens sake. Seven to ten years I told her, that's what you could have got if someone had stopped you or if they were on to her waiting to see where the cash was going to end up, to see where the drugs were going. Realistically she wasn't out of it yet. I asked her how much a year she thought it would be worth if she'd been caught. Less than two hundred a year. It just didn't make sense.

Before all of this and my trip to Holland I'd never met an international drug smuggler apart from Campbell or a lad who I met clubbing who told me that he'd taken a couple of dozen pills to Ibiza with him in a sealed 35mm plastic film case which he'd shoved with some considerable discomfort up his bum. He thought that it would be easier than putting them in a condom because if that broke then he'd be high for ages. Someone had told him that taking an E like a suppository increases its efficiency. The other draw back he saw with a condom was that pills had to be strong enough not crumble in your pocket and soft enough to dissolve quickly in the stomach. The hundreds of illegal pill makers obviously hadn't given enough thought to how their expensive product might have been carried. I'd told him that I thought he was crazy because the airports today had scanners which were specifically designed to pick up plastics after the use of plastic explosives at Lockerbie. He didn't seem to perturbed and retorted that he thought that most of the systems operated by finding imbalances in what they scanned and that he was confident that he could and indeed had, adjusted his balance accordingly. He might not have been stopped but it had hardly seemed worth it as he'd had a pretty sore bum for the first few days of his holiday

I should have shut up and just comforted her but I was so upset that she'd done something so stupid without telling me about it. I didn't want to think of her languishing in a foreign jail, let alone an English one. I couldn't cope with that and Summer really worried me because I had no idea if she knew what she was getting herself into.

"You should have told me. You should of told me." I yelled at her.

She said that Campbell said that she didn't have any choice in the matter. "Baba, you know what he's like, I'm scared and he's arranging for me to do it again."

"There's no fucking way," I shouted getting to my feet. "No fucking way."

"But its all arranged, you've heard what he does to people who mess him around. I'm really scared, I don't need the money but I am really scared that he's going to hurt me, Baba."

"Well we'll see about this. You'll have to give me the money for a start, we cannot have that littering up your flat or just appearing in one of your bank accounts tomorrow. Has he said when he wants you to do the next trip?"

"In a few weeks, this time its the Grand Cayman. That was his idea when I told him that my cousin lived there. He says that I should stay with her and it will be less suspicious."

"Well it'll give me sometime to think about it all. You do realise that every time you go through those Customs channels the closer you are to spending a very long time in Holloway and when I say Holloway I don't mean the Sign of the Times Club. The man must be stupid, there are millions of easier ways of getting goods into the country than airports, it's almost as if he's trying to get caught."

She pulled her arms around me and sunk her head into my shoulders and began to sob. I'd said enough. I just held her and racked my brains as what I could do to get her out of this. I felt responsible for introducing her to the clubbing scene and for obviously not being approachable enough for her to tell me exactly what was going on before it happened. I ran scenario after scenario through my head. I remembered what Steve had told me about Campbell being totally ruthless. I'd have to careful but at the moment there didn't seem an alternative other than her going back and taking her chances. We didn't have any bargaining power and I certainly wasn't equipped to employ force. I'd come in from the cold and here I was a couple of months on, up to my eyes in it, one way or other it was all getting out of control. A couple of Es a week well that was child's play compared with all of the added extras I'd got myself lumbered with. Everyone had heard stories of the supposed eminence griece of the dance music scene, it was just my luck to get tangled up with him. Why couldn't I be like all the other clubbers that I met, all they seemed to do was drop lots of pills and have the time of their lives. My desire to get the most out of the scene had definitely started to back fire, I'd been far too greedy and had moved miles away from the initial happiness and non egotistical spirit that I'd warmed to so much.

If this wasn't enough I had work to keep on top of and I still had to do all of the preparation for "Well Mobbed." E itself wasn't causing me a problem but all of the late nights were eating in to the week and gnawing away at my cutting edge. There was only one thing to do and to lay off it for the next couple of weeks. Of course come Friday, I'd get that Friday feeling, where everything rushes past as the adrenaline starts to pump in preparation for the night or weekend ahead. It wasn't a physical thing though and I knew that despite getting geared up for the night out that it wasn't a sign of dependency, that it was just the same type of rush that anticipates a Cup Final or a special occasion. Leaving it for a few weeks wouldn't be a problem.

Summer cried herself to sleep. I didn't feel like going to work but I had to keep on track, I'd decided that last night. Summer was still out of it as I left in the morning. She didn't ring during the day. Jet lag was only one of the many factors that kept her in bed. I made sure that I didn't forget to visit the safe deposit box on the way to work. It was getting quite full now, what with Steve's cash, my pills and now Summer's drug running money. Later that day at work I engrossed myself in a plan to get Summer out of the mess she'd been dragged into. I made tons of 'phone calls and was certain that I'd be able to pull it off, I just had to make sure that Campbell didn't find out what I was up to.

Occasionally I'd brighten up the flat with a couple of bunches of flowers. Bold colours, long stems and not too much diversity of colour. Not any of these mixed bunches or cheap roses you saw on the stalls in the tube stations or at the side of the main arterial roads. I was a Colombia Row or a Berwick Street market man. I didn't buy flowers for anyone else. Summer was an exception, she managed her first post smuggling smile as I handed her a mountain of flowers that I'd got from Brick Lane at lunch time. I persuaded her that we should go out for dinner. She only agreed if she could wear my wrap around sun glasses. They cheered her up, hid her tired blood shot eyes and provided good entertainment value as she picked herself up dancing round her small flat looking at herself in each of the mirrors. She needed to build up her spirits and confidence for what lay ahead.

Dinner had to be somewhere different, somewhere I hadn't been before. There was nothing like a change to get the brain working again. I needed to get as far away as possible from Campbell's empire. That ruled out Soho and we ended up in the Chop House just South of Tower Bridge. Huge place, fabulously busy. We sat and ate but weren't up to sitting in there all evening. It wasn't the ambience of the restaurant, we just found it difficult to relax, to forget what was being planned around us.

We just wanted to be together, just the two of us. We drifted along the illuminated Esplanade, marvelling at the architectural cheesecake of Tower Bridge. We watched the reflections dance in the waves, followed the barges and yachts as they made their way up and down the river in the moon light. I knew how we were going to get around Campbell plans and I gently told her exactly how it was going to happen. There was something refreshing about the Thames as it flowed benevolently and seemingly benignly past us, quietly washing along the shore beneath the deserted embankment.

Summer and I made it to Glastonbury but only for the Saturday night. Everyone else had gone for the long weekend and came back with stories of epic sets from Carl Cox and Danny Rampling. We would have stayed longer but Summer was so wound up with everything that was going on around her, I can't say that I blame her. We were lucky in that we didn't have to pay to get in, there was a huge hole in the steel fence and while I didn't mind paying it was quite a thrill to get in for free. Glastonbury offered great value for money in a sharp contrast to a lot of so called special events which charged twenty or thirty quid for what effectively was the privilege of dancing with your girlfriend in a bus shelter. It was fun watching the crowds and deciding who was on the beer and who was on the E. Those dancing and hugging each other were on the pills and those sitting, groping and snogging in the sunshine were on the beer.

Summer tried to take a picture of a local fire engine decked out with its crew driving slowly across one of the large open fields. She made the mistake of framing a rather large irate drugs dealer in the process, it was only me appealing to his friends better judgement which meant that she left intact with her camera. We didn't need hassles like that, not at anytime.

To cheer her up I took her to Jon Pleased Wimmins Wednesday night extravaganza at the Velvet Underground. It was one of the best small clubs in London where they'd spent a few pennies on decent decor, a thumping good sound system and even loo paper, hand basins and mirrors in the cubicles. Jon was a real scream, a larger than life glamour trannie who played brilliant in your face underground house beats. Summer had met him before at a 'Georgies' party at a

It's Our Future

West London film studio and persuaded him to sign the back of a photo I'd taken of the two of them. I don't know whether it was the embarrassment of all the unexpected attention or the memory of Summer accidentally knocking the record decks at Georgie's that brought a blush to the face of the normally unblushing Jon. What seemed to make Jon's evening when Summer told him that he was even better than Jeremy Healy. Jon said words to the effect of, "well I know that anyway" but I could tell that he was really chuffed, well pleased if you like.

It was refreshing to get back and hear from Tony, He'd been away for ages, far longer than the month he initially anticipated, business had gone really well and he was thinking of relocating somewhere in the burgeoning economies of the Pacific.

We spent an afternoon in his Hammersmith flat. Its glass fronted windows overlooked the Thames and the Harrods Furniture Depositry. He'd decorated it with art and sculpture by contemporary artists. He was amazed to hear of the extent to which I'd got into the scene and was impressed with the idea of 'Well Mobbed'. I had a go on his Technics and found out just how hard it is to get started. Tony showed me how it was done, there was no way that I could turn down his request to play at Well Mobbed, after all if it hadn't been for him then there was no way that it would have taken off in the first place. I was careful not to tell Tony everything, I didn't know how he'd react to any of my dealing stories and Summers problems were best kept quiet.

It's Our Future

Tony had caught quite a tan on his travels, it reminded me that I still hadn't been away properly. There wasn't time just yet but it was top of my list of priorities.

I arranged to see Steve to sort out the pill business for 'Well Mobbed' I would have gone down to see him but he insisted in driving up to London. He brought his Dad with him and I didn't really know what to say. Steve's dad was a big friendly Geordie and it transpired that he'd come up to town with Steve to keep him company because he was still missing Jules. We drove around for a while and Steve told his dad to wait in the car as the two of us went for a walk. His dad knew about the pill business but he wasn't involved himself, he knew that his lad had to make a decent living one way or another. Steve told me later that on the way back to Kent that his dad had given him a clip around the ear because he thought that Steve had been selling me pills. If only he knew exactly what was going on.

....

The Criminal Justice and Public Order Act 1995 was a rat bag collection of laws, it lowered the age of consent for homosexuals but left it higher than for heterosexuals. It introduced new laws on trespass, allowed for stiffer penalties for grave offences and it placed a requirement on party organisers to get a licence or face large fines and confiscation of their equipment. It was the latter which had really cheesed most people off. It led to marches, rallies and riots against it's implementation. It really just tightened up the law, adding a new piece of weaponry against the party goer. It wasn't really needed. If the

It's Our Future

Police wanted to stop parties they could get the environmental health departments to prosecute for excess noise. Prosecute for nuisance and or criminal damage to the areas used, or just evoke the various provisions of the Public Order Act. The new Act was just a way of dressing up the old powers in a different guise, one which would catch the public eye, win a few votes and persuade people that something was being done to protect our citizens against the wilder elements of our society who just want to enjoy themselves by partying all weekend long.

The Act had introduced swingeing penalties for those who didn't comply with it. Everyone in club land had a licence, they were almost as in important as a good DJ. It was only the smaller underground events that got away without a licence. If you were on the High Street, well, it was time to go legal.

James and I instructed a firm of Solicitors, 'Atkins, Saunderson and May' to help us persuade Wells Street Magistrates Court that we deserved a licence. Our bottom line was that we were two professional gentlemen, putting on a well financed, safe and secure dance extravaganza. We wanted to lend it an air of responsibility. For experience we got Steve's brother to give us strength in depth with his organisational experience. Then there was Super Foods Plc. Their backing was to prove crucial. In addition to the six a.m. dance licence, we needed at least a two a.m. alcohol licence. There were still people out there who drank the stuff and unashamedly we wanted their money.

It's Our Future

I'd been to the solicitors office to outline our case and tell them what we wanted. I was a little surprised that when we got to Court the solicitor had instructed a barrister who I'd never met before but who assured me that he knew exactly what we wanted. He said that the only problem, that he could foresee was that the premises were not covered by planning permission for this type of thing and that there was residential property close by. He was relatively optimistic stating however that nothing was ever certain at law. There were objectors but that was nothing unusual for this type of application To counter these we had included in our proposals that the one street with houses on it should be blocked off by security with access for residents only. We were even going to give the locals a few free tickets. Parking we were able to provide on the hanger sized street level of the premises so that wasn't going to be a problem.

At first I wasn't too happy about being allocated a barrister. I thought that my solicitor would know more about the case given the large amount of expensive time that we'd spent with him discussing it. Counsel was a short balding man with glasses. He told us that we wouldn't be on at the allotted time because the Court always listed everything at the same time. He said we'd be nearer one o'clock than ten o'clock but that he'd see if the usher could try to get us on earlier. That obviously back fired as they told us to come back after two o'clock. At least Steve's brother might be here by then, He'd rung me on the mobile to say that he was having a few difficulties in getting into town.

It's Our Future

Counsel seemed as glum as us at the news. He made the excuse about checking something in Pattersons, pointing to a thick book which he had somewhat proudly and ostentaciuosly displayed like a badge of office all day, perhaps as if to make up for the fact that he wasn't wearing a wig or gown, such not being required in the magistrates court. James and I adjourned to a local street cafe, there was no point in waiting at the Court, the atmosphere was depressing and the prospect of spending the next three or four hours just sitting there staring at the broken, instant coffee machine didn't appeal a lot.

I knew of a street corner cafe not too far away under the shadow of the Telecom Tower. We sat out in the summer heat, ordering pastries and cupaccinos. My purposeless stare was interrupted when I realised that I was looking at someone and they were looking back at me. Not just anyone, it was Campbell. I tried to avert my gaze and pretend that he wasn't there. I looked back again as if by instinct for confirmation. He was sitting there dressed as ever in a loose vest that showed off his well developed shoulder, chest and arm muscles. He wore a bandanna out of which his pony tail flowed from the rear. He looked relaxed and in control. He forced a wry smile as he saw me looking at him.

I tried to look away again, perhaps I was just imagining it. It wasn't a flash back, bad dream or a trick of my imagination. Perhaps I should just pretend that I didn't know who he was and hurry off to the quasi sanctuary of the court precincts. There wasn't time though. He lifted his considerable frame out of the chair and was coming round in my direction. Shit, he was coming for me. I just sat there frozen with fear.

"What?" enquired James puzzled at my odd behaviour. His remark was cut short by the appearance of the intimidating figure of Campbell.

"Just be cool." I muttered. I wasn't sure whether I was talking to James or myself.

He sat down next to us. "Well gentlemen. You will not mind if I join you, will you? After all we're in the same business aren't we. It would be rude of me not to welcome fellow promoters to the club scene. You'll have heard of my clubs, he reeled off four of the biggest names in London clubland, places that I avoided like the plague. "We are glad to welcome new business as long as they fit into the scheme of things. I am sure that you're going to get along well, you see if I thought that you couldn't fit in then I would have had to have gone to the Court and told them that I thought that your club wouldn't be good for clubland and you wouldn't have got your licence. No I think that you will run your club in a proper manner so that we all can benefit. I am the brand leader in this business and as I see it all imitation is a form of flattery. But...," His voice slowed in pace and increased in intensity. "You must pay royalties. I will be there to see how you do and then we will talk about how we can improve things for you." There were sixty or so clubs in London and he'd decided to pick on ours.

James was sitting there. I could see him fighting between saying, "who the hells this, or that's it I am off and the partys off."

It's Our Future

"Gentlemen you will have a good party and I am sure that you will get all the help you need in planning more parties. After all you know that in this business you need a little bit of co-operation and help from your friends if your not going to run into problems." He held out his hand I had to stand and shake it. Shit, he knew about me and he knew about Summer, he was going to have a cut of the two of us. What did he mean about sorting out things after the first party, did he want control of the drugs market, was it the door takings and did it mean that he wasn't wanting a share of the first event? Did he expect us just to become part of his empire?

I should have asked him what he was on about. Well I couldn't, could I? He hadn't mentioned anything directly and from that I knew about him I didn't want to appear impolite. I could have mentioned words like drugs and protection but I thought that I'd offend him by mentioning such dirty words. No they might be the bread and butter of his existence but no it wouldn't do to mention them. The ball was well and truly in his court and it was up to him to make things clearer if and when he wanted to.

"Gentlemen, I must be going now, I wish you the best of luck with their worships. You'll have no problems, I've seen to that."

He decanted his huge frame into a large Mercedes parked just across the road. It must have been there all the time, it was replete with his usual crowd of hanger ons.

I almost smirked to myself. There he was one of the most dangerous men in London and he'd chosen to dress

like a South American drugs dealer, running round in a
flashy souped up car with a group of henchmen. I
thought that men in his position didn't have to hanker
after all the trimmings and look just like the next gangster
on the block. Wasn't he smart enough to realise that he
could do without all the attention he was drawing to
himself. The Police would know who he was anyway but
I was sure that he'd be able to run his business better if he
was a little more discrete, a little less obvious. After all
I'd only got to know about who he was by seeing him at
all of the clubs field marshalling his troops around.

"Who the fucks your mate?" It was understating
matters to say James wasn't too happy about Campbell's
visit. He sounded extremely perturbed and upset. "You
know shit like that and you don't tell me. I thought that
you'd told me all there was to know about this game.
They're not the fucking geezers that Steve was telling you
about are they?"

"Yeah its them and that's why we've got to go through
with this if we stop now then they'll see that as a slight
and we wouldn't want to upset them. Its the first time
that I've spoken to the geezer. I would have told you if
I'd thought that he was going to interfere but you could
probably tell from what he was saying or rather what he
wasn't saying that we hadn't been introduced, I've seen
him, acting like a gangster and the words obviously out
on the grapevine that we're planning something. I'd risk a
guess that he doesn't want the door money and that he's
not really going to influence our musical direction. What
he wants is our drug trade and if we've got no plans to
organise that ourselves then   he's probably doing us a

favour, besides I'd rather have the top firm doing it than some middle ranking Johnny come lately who'd just attract the likes of Campbell in the long run. Anyhow, I lied we were both respectable professional men who've made a decision not to get further involved in drugs after that little episode in my flat with Lewis' chemistry set.

I'd convinced myself of the logic of it all. I just had to convince James, there was no way that I could lose him now. And there was the problem of my three thousand little tablets. I couldn't tell anyone else about them, they were my secret and if all went to plan then I'd be able to off load on the first night. I was certain that Campbell had suggested that we had a clear run on the first night, but I had to do it without treading on his feet.

"This is your fucking idea. Once its up and running that's it I am out of it there's no way I am sticking around to get crap off some South American gangster running round like he owns the show." James had had enough.

"Listen, I totally agree. At least he'll be on our side so to speak, he won't be ripping down our posters and giving the kids who hand out our flyers a hard time. There's nothing we can do about it, we cannot get the police on to him, he's too clever for that, they wouldn't be able to help and there's no way that we could muscle him out of it. No we've just got to go along with it."

Time went slowly as we waited to go back to court. I should have expected something like this. There had been no violence, no real threats, nothing spelt out in black and white but it was obvious that he felt that he could walk straight on to the stage and pick up a large pay cheque for doing next to nothing. He didn't have to do anything it was his reputation that did the work for him. He was Mr Big in his own eyes and in this particular field there was no doubting that he was Mr Big Enough.

To make matters worse counsels efforts to get us on early in the afternoon had back fired again. James suggested that we go to a particular Soho cafe. No I said, that's owned by Campbell from what I've heard. No we might be letting him in to our project there was no way that I was going to line his pockets yet again. Paranoia that he might have a hand in any number of local establishments meant that we stayed in the courts precincts for the best part of the afternoon.

I told James to relax and try to see the funny side of it after all he was the practical joker and he was the one who in a couple of months, if all went well would be making light of today. Maybe in a couple of months but not today, that was for sure. He seriously questioned whether at the rate things were moving whether he'd have grandchildren never mind be round to tell them about this.

We had to wait behind a pub licence which was opposed by the Police on the grounds that it caused them and the local hospital too much trouble at the weekends. The chairwoman was the lady who'd been round to visit our premises to check their suitability. She'd seemed to be on our side. Counsel in a rare slip of mask mentioned that in his opinion that she was mutton dressed as lamb and that she looked on young male licensees favourably.

"Number seventy Four, Madam," announced the usher.

We were led round to the witness box and counsel addressed the bench as to the nature of our application.

203

It's Our Future

"Madam I understand that there are objectors in this case."

"No, that was the case but they were withdrawn over the short adjournment." Lunchtime, she meant and there was a feeling of dread in my stomach as I ran through the possible reasons, either they'd got bored of waiting or someone had had a word with them. Counsel went onto make our application. I was thinking of Campbell when I was called to give my evidence.

"Counsel if you wouldn't mind I'll take this young man through his evidence."

"I am grateful Madam."

"So can you confirm that you know who you can serve alcohol, who you're not allowed to serve alcohol to and who would be disqualified from holding a licence."

I gave her the standard answers from what I'd gleaned from my solicitor and barrister. She probed me for a little more background as to what type of event it was that we were actually wanting to put on.

"Well, its mainly for the eighteen to twenty five year olds, its a dance extravaganza, we've got thirty stewards to help organise the evening it's not the type of event where we'd expect any trouble from the punters. we've got two main dance floors and an area where people can just sit and rest. There's a first aid post." She cut me short before I could finish.

"What about drugs, ecstasy, I mean?" Well that caught me by surprise, I retorted.

"We have a very firm policy on drugs. Security will search them thoroughly. They're trained to know what to look for and anyone caught will be ejected from the premises and the Police informed. I've arranged with the Police for them to visit the premises immediately prior to the event so that they can be assured that there are no illegal substances there. I believe that this is common practice and I am prepared to co-operate one hundred percent with the Police on this particular issue."

"Thank you I am grateful that you've had the forethought to look into these issues, there does seem to be a problem in a lot of the clubs that I visit. Strangely however I rarely get Police complaints or objections for this type of thing but you need to be fully aware of what could be going on.

Steve's brother didn't turn up and remarkably the Magistrate said that this didn't matter because she knew him from a licence he held for a different club.

She asked James the usual questions but thankfully nothing too demanding. He wasn't up to that just now.

"Well thank you gentlemen it was most refreshing to speak to you both, I have no hesitation in granting this licence and wish you every success with your venture."

Outside the Court counsel looked rather relieved and before he scampered off he congratulated us on our victory. That was one of the hurdles out of the way. The juggernaut was beginning to inch its way into place.

....

Summer should have arrived back at just before midday but it wasn't until just after four o'clock that I got a 'phone call. It wasn't Summer, it was some one from Heathrow Police Station. Would I take a call from

It's Our Future

Summer? Shit, was she all right? What had happened? There were too many questions and I didn't want her answering any of them from a Police Station. She was going to be remanded in custody until Monday morning when they'd take her to Uxbridge Magistrates Court. I told her that I loved her and that it would be okay, there wasn't much else to say was there?

I busied myself with the evenings arrangements. At least there was something to do. Something to keep my mind off what had gone wrong.

James and Tony came round to the flat as arranged. I didn't tell them about Summer, there was nothing that we could do now. I didn't want to spoil the electric atmosphere that they were emitting. We all agreed that there'd be no drugs or alcohol when we were working. James said that we were acting like conquering heroes, when all we were was a group of professional men playing childish games. That was the point though as I saw it. This scene was all about sheer hedonism and for most people their childhood and late teens is the happiest times of their lives, we were simply reliving it and making sure that we didn't get too old before our time. We all agreed that the buzz was as good as necking an E and congratulated ourselves on our natural high.

We got to the premises early to supervise the installation of the sound and lights. That took forever, I didn't realise exactly what was involved but at least it was all done in time. I'd arrange a meeting before we opened with Inspector Grant. He took a chair in what we were using as the main office, he seemed quite impressed with the set up and asked whether we were agreeable to him visiting on the next occasion. Of course I was. I was trying to stay on the right side of the Police. I'd had quite alot of contact with them, one thing or another since finding the coke in Summers bag. Normally out of choice I wouldn't go within a million miles of the Police but I'd have to use every available option if I was going to get us out of this mess.

Just as we were going to go and fetch the rest of his officers to allow them to conduct a drugs search on the premises, the door to the office burst open. It was Campbell with James in close pursuit. He stopped when he saw the Inspector. Definitely not like Campbell, he normally knew all of what went on.

The Inspector did the talking. "Well, what a surprise to see you here, just checking out the opposition I hope. Was there anything which I could help you with?"

Campbell, looked wrong footed, stumped for something to say. His eyes scored their gaze on mine, he wasn't entirely sure of what was going on and why I had the Police there, he was trying to suss me out. The Inspector intervened and said that he was going to invite his dog handling officers in to do the search. That seemed to clinch it. It was a routine visit, no we weren't talking about him and he had nothing to worry about. Campbell said that he was leaving and made his way out muttering something along the lines about wanting to do business with the gentleman but that he was busy."

I asked James to give him a business card and to see him out. I don't think James saw the funny side of this.

I dodged my way round the springer spaniels as they raced through the venue, either looking for drugs or showing an allergic reaction to the thumping Detriot Tony was mixing from the decks. I hoped that there were no traces of anything left in my pockets I could do without being eaten by a hungry, drug crazed doggie.

The rest of the evening went so quickly, there was so much to do with supervising the door, making sure that the DJs were running on time, ensuring that the VIP room was okay and that the DJs riders were in order. Socialising with all of the right people and telling them all that I didn't know where Summer was but that I hoped that she would turn up sooner or later.

Then of course there was Steve and Co to liaise with. I'd got him in round the back, with his staff posing as a DJ and flunkies. The gear came in a couple of large well stickered DJ record boxes which I'd given him two weeks previously. It certainly wasn't an original idea but I couldn't be bothered getting them to bring it in pizza boxes or whatever besides surely no one would have thought that people still brought large amounts of pills into a club in DJ boxes, that was as old as the summer of love itself. I could trust Steve, he was reliable as drugs dealers go, more to the point he was a mate. The arrangement was that Steve would cash his team up every hour and that he'd slip the cash to me. The pills went really quickly, he reckoned that we'd be out of them by two or three o'clock and that was about the time that most people would want some more if they were going on till six. He'd suggested putting up the price of what we had left but I wasn't too keen on that, there was no point, people might not pay it and we didn't want them going away thinking that we were overpriced and not coming back again.

Steve said that he could make a few calls on his mobile and see what he could buy. I told him that as long as he made sure that they were good stuff that I didn't want a cut of them, he'd been pretty good to me all along. If he hadn't organised selling my stuff then I'd still have a pile of three thousand pills burning a hole in my safety deposit box. I worked out that I'd made twenty seven grand on the pills. That was selling them to the crowd for fifteen quid a go and less three quid to Steve and minus three quid purchase price. Not bad for a nights work I thought.

James wasn't too sure about it though, he'd prised himself away from a group of young girls who'd been happy to sit and drink champagne with him in the V.I.P room, waiting for one of the DJs. He'd seen Steve of course and gone absolutely mental. I managed to calm him down with the promise of the cut of my takings. That helped a little but I could see he wasn't happy with me for going behind his back. If I'd asked him he would have said no and there was no way that we could have run the evening as well with out Steve helping the night along. I reassured him that there was nothing to link him with Steve and that the Police had been and gone, it wasn't as if they were going to raid us on our first night. If they'd wanted to they could have objected to our application for a licence. No the Polices attitude seemed to be that they knew that large scale dealing went on in clubs and that unless they applied for a search warrant they were powerless to enter the premises.

It's Our Future

There were so many clubs in London that there was no way that they could raid them all. No whilst the Police wouldn't publicly admit that they were not enforcing the drugs laws the plain facts were that apart from the occasional well publicised raid on the likes of Club UK, which had unfairly come in for such a level of intervention. Other than picking on certain establishments and inviting the media along to film the process there was no way that they had the man power or the resolve to raid every club where they thought, rightly or wrongly, that dealing went on. They really had two alternatives and that was to turn a blind eye to the problem or to try to close all the clubs that had effectively opened as a response to the swinging laws on out door raves. No it suited them to have parties where they knew were they were, parties which they knew would be well organised and trouble free. It must have been a tremendous relief for Police forces up and down the country as clubs began to set up where there were no problems with violent disorder and the associated problems of the old alcohol based culture.

We'd made forty five grand on the door and a small fortune from the cloakroom and sale of soft drinks. I was surprised that we'd also notched up pretty high sales of alcohol. I'd made arrangements with Safe Bank to pick up the bulk of the takings. Of course the DJs and staff wanted paying in cash but I was careful to plan ahead so that we weren't walking out first thing in the morning with huge amounts of cash in our pockets, I'd remembered reading about another club in Victoria being held up and robbed after closing time,   well that wasn't going to happen here, we were prepared this week and next time we'd have the added protection of dear old Campbell, no one in their right mind would try to get in his way. Given our run away success I'd be able to give Lewis what he owed the bank, he needed the cash more than me at the moment.

For me the biggest thrill of the evening was going on to the dance floor and watching everyone around me going absolutely wild knowing that I'd helped in some way. It was a wonderful feeling just being there and thinking that it was my party and it was going really well.

Steve didn't seem too happy when I told him that the next event might have different line management on the dealing side. I said that I'd put a word in for him, so he'd get the contract so to speak. He worked for Campbell's rivals once and was a little worried that there might be a problem.

It was good to see everyone there. Greg had made a come back, we'd lost him to the beers over the last few months. Jeff had a big one and Lewis his girlfriend and Claire all turned up. Everyone else went on somewhere after we'd finished but I'd had my fun, I wanted to quit while I was ahead, there were still quite a lot to be done before Monday morning and Summers court appearance. That was the most important thing on my mind at the moment.

....

Uxbridge was waking up when I arrived just before eight on the Monday morning. I'd tried to stay at home and leave at a proper time but I wasn't sure what time the Court opened and I thought that there might be a chance to see Summer as she was brought to the Court. The Court was actually open but the security staff told me that there was hardly any point in being there until nine thirty when people normally started to arrive. They directed me to McDonalds which was just round the corner.

I didn't have much of an appetite but I managed a big breakfast as I sat reading the mornings papers. I couldn't see anything about Summer but then again it seemed only to be the larger hauls which the national press bothered with today, unless of course it was ecstasy related and then the confiscation of a couple of tablets was front page news. I sat and bided my time wondering how she was coping.

I started to get up but sat down with as a feeling of sheer terror over took me, it was Campbell. A grinning, laughing Campbell who had walked in through the doors with two of his cronies. They were resplendent in their uniform of vests and bandannas and were heading in my direction.

"Good morning, I hear that Saturday night was a success." he said extending his hand in greeting.

I stood half up and took hold of his hand as a matter of instinct. I didn't want to do it but with Campbell you had no choice.

"There's no reason to stand,"

"Yes." I said tying to keep a grip on myself, to keep calm and not to let him see more than was already apparent of my nerves.

It's Our Future

"Your girl is a good girl. You should be proud of her but she has caused some problems and no doubt by the virtue of the fact that you are here you will know what they are. The Customs have got something which does not belong to them. That can not be helped now but it is a tragedy that they will not know what to do with the consignment, they will burn it, that will be a terrible waste. A tragedy."

"What about Summer," I asked him? "She's in prison, she's only twenty five, I cannot see her serving time she just wouldn't be up to it would she?

"I know don't worry there are things which can happen in cases like this, I can help. You probably think that I am annoyed that my cargo didn't come through but the very nature of my business is risk. I take them and I take the consequences. No I'm not very happy but I can help her."

I just looked at him no response, no expression, I decided to let him do the talking.

"She's been good to me once before. I take the logical view in business, what I have made on that deal I can afford to lose on this one I am still a long way ahead. She has two options at the moment. The first is to get bail and disappear somewhere out of the country. The second is to deny that she knew of what was with her in her bags. He said that he had ten thousand pounds which I could use as a bail surety. He had it there in his pocket. He looked at me straight in the eyes and reminded me that he had his own special surety in the form of our business arrangement which started next month. He wanted co-operation on that, as if he wouldn't get it I thought to myself. He mentioned out of passing that should there be any silly talk as he put it that we could find ourselves in big trouble. He had as much on me as I had on him. He probably actually knew more about my business than I knew about his. Never mind that there was no way that I was going to be caught crossing Campbell.

"I'll be in touch," he said turning to his friends and ushering them out of the restaurant. the white Mercedes was outside the front door and in attendance was a young traffic warden. She handed Campbell a parking ticket, he gestured extending both of his hands with his palms out as if to say what have I done, he shrugged his shoulders and put an one around the warden and with his free hand gave her what appeared to be a fifty pound note. He got back in the car and the traffic warden just stood there with an incredulous look on her face. She composed herself and put the note and the ticket under the Mercedes large single sweep windscreen wiper.

Campbell had that type of effect on people. Most of the restaurant were engrossed in his attempts to charm the warden. It was all part of his image. He didn't want a ticket, what would it cost £10, £20, £'0? that didn't matter, what he wanted to do was to pay it there and then. What do you mean I cannot pay it now? Here's £50 keep the change I am not concerned about breaking your little laws and I'll pay to get around them, there was no way that he wanted to be caught traversing the law even on the most minor matter.

As he drove off normality was restored, at least I thought that it had been restored, I saw that half of the restaurant were looking at me and it wasn't necessarily because I'd been speaking to him neither was it because I had a suit on, no the huddle of lawyers in the corner were wearing suits, no it was the £10,000 which he had dumped on the table. He'd told me about it but I'd been so wrapped up that I hadn't notice him put the surety money on the table. It was in loose £50 notes. I gathered it quickly and put as much as I could into my breast pocket and folded the rest into my copy of the Times. I got up with a sniff and a shrug as if to say what's unusual about sitting in a fast food restaurant with £10,000 on the table? Haven't you seen money before. I made my way back purposefully the hundred or so yards to the Court. I didn't care who'd seen the money I was sure that it was safe with me, it was Campbells money and no one was going to touch that if they were in their right minds.

Summer had arrived in one of what Security described as sweat boxes. Charming it was good to see that prisons had moved into the twentieth century. I wasn't able to see her there were no personal visits to the cells and in any case her barrister and solicitor were with her.

Ten thirty came and went. I tried to find out which Court she was in . "Court One luvvie," said the friendly usher with a slight hint of a Liverpool accent, "are you a friend?" she asked me.

"Yeah."

"Well she's represented by a Mr Molby, from 'Walton, Kemlyn and Breck' Solicitors. They wanted a bit of time, the last time that I spoke to them. Do they know that you're here?"

It's Our Future

"Should do but I haven't spoken to anyone but could you pass a message on that I am in a position to stand a substantial surety."

"Okay, luvvie."

I sat on the hard plastic seats in the midst of the acrid cigarette smoke for what seemed to be an age. There were kids everywhere, one or two of them looked as if they might go to UK or somewhere like that. The rest were a sartorial mess. Not the practical, ordered, deliberate mess of a traveller or of the 'dirty, smelly, all weekend raver'. They wore a repulsive array of ill fitting garishly coloured and poorly cut clothes off set with an array of poorly executed hand made tattoos, poor dentistry, inadequate diet and a total lack of self respect. They sat, smoked and acted the fool. Most of them hadn't left the classroom actually or metaphorically. They were only occasionally diverted by the solemn dark suited lawyers, assigned to them doubtlessly as a damage limitation exercise.

I decided to sit in Court One for a while. There were three Magistrates sitting with a clerk sitting in front of them. It was the clerk who seemed to be running the proceedings, dictating who spoke when, addressing the prosecution, defence and magistrates alike.

Most of the cases were simply put off to other dates, three of four weeks in the future. nothing was dealt with there and then. The clerk announced that the court would be retiring for fifteen minutes, until eleven thirty. It was their mid morning tea break. As far as I could make out they hadn't actually done anything to warrant a tea break, but there we were. At least it might put them in a more relaxed mood when they came to Summer.

The usher who'd spoken to me earlier was talking to a tall blonde colleague as I left the Court. She caught my eye and called me over saying that Summers solicitor had just requested that I go down to the cell areas to discuss some aspects of the case.

I thanked her and made my way in the direction she pointed.

I wasn't actually allowed into the cell area. Summers barrister introduced himself to me and we walked to where he said that we should be able to get a consultation room.We passed a large queue for tea and coffee and went into a small smoke filled room. We left the door open slightly ajar to get some air, but closed enough to get some privacy from the hoards who were waiting outside.

"She's bearing up well considering. " He said

"Has she made any statements or given interview to the police?" I asked with concern.

"She's adamant that she knew nothing about it, that she didn't pack her own bag and before she flew that there was nothing of the sort in there. She says that some of her things are missing from her bag and is suggesting that whoever put the cocaine in her bag took out her belongings so that the weight difference wouldn't have been noticed."

"So, they can't pin anything on her?"

Well it's not as simple as that." He said drawing forwards over the small Formica table. Its a serious charge and they're not going to drop it on that basis, this will probably go all the way to trial. You're right though as long as she's consistent with what she says then she's got a good chance, but all of this takes a long time you understand."

"What about bail?"

"I am not too hopeful, we can try but given the likely sentence if the prosecution prove their case, and we would be talking years here, as I say I am not too hopeful."

"She's got everything in her favour though, surely, good job, stable background, and as I told the usher I can stand as a surety.."

"How much? He asked, obviously the message hadn't got through.

"Anything you want, up to £30,000, whatever you think is appropriate."

"Well, I am not sure whether they'll want that much but I'll have a word with my learned friend for the prosecution." He sounded more hopeful now. "The only problem though with sureties in this type of case is that they often draw an assumption that sureties are often tainted with drugs money. Summer tells me though that you're a partner in a firm of City Accountants."

"Not exactly a partner, not quite, not yet and not ever if all of this seeps back to the office, if it does then I'll probably have to find a job as a tea boy somewhere. No seriously I can vouch for her character if they want to hear somebody on that side of things."

"Thank you," he said non committally.

"Is there any chance of seeing her before all of this goes ahead?"

It's Our Future

"'fraid not. Hopefully you'll get every opportunity afterwards, but as I said I have my reservations about that and you mustn't build up your hopes. If they don't grant bail then I can get her solicitor to help you arrange visits to Holloway or wherever it is where they take them from here. As I understand it they're pretty relaxed about remand visits there."

Thanks, I thought.

"You'd better do your level best on this one, from what I've heard remand visiting is normally just in office time and a mans got to work hasn't he." I joked nervously.

I got out the £10,000 from Campbell, I'd never seen such a look of horror as came over his came over his face.

"Put that away, I haven't seen it, I won't ask where it came from so don't tell me."

"Don't worry, I supplement my salary with a legitimate business venture once a month and its just that I haven't banked the takings yet. Its all legal," I said, which was true, I suppose.

Well whatever just keep it in your pocket if the court sees that then they'll have you down as a member of a Colombian drugs cartel and they won't have to give much thought to all of this bail business."

Summer was flanked by two large guards resplendent in green uniforms. It was good to see her. She looked tired and was visibly upset. She looked briefly in my direction and managed half a smile.

She agreed with the Court Clerk that the name and address read out were hers.

It's Our Future

A besuited gentleman stood up at the front of the Court and addressed the magistrates, "May it please you sir, I understand from my learned friend that there is to be a bail application in this case. It will be opposed by Her Majesties Customs and Excise. The brief facts of the case are that Customs officers stopped the Defendant as she disembarked from a flight from Gran Cayman on Saturday evening last. She had proceeded through the Green channel with her reclaimed baggage. Customs officers examined the contents of her suitcase and found it to contain approximately five kilograms of cocaine. She was duly arrested and is before you today. In view of the amount of drugs concerned the prosecution would oppose bail fearful that the Defendant would fail to surrender and also being mindful of the likely nature and length of sentence."

Summers barrister stood up and addressed the Court. "Sir I am grateful to my learned friend for Her Majesties Customs and Excise, for his concise rendition of the facts as they are before you today, he has omitted several pertinent factors which I shall seek to bring to the attention of the Court. My client is a woman of twenty five years and of good character. She has been interviewed in respect of this matter on several occasions and her responses to the questions asked are consistent. She has fully co-operated with the Police but she is unable to assist them any further in this matter as she does not know how the goods in question came to be in her possession. There is no forensic evidence that I am aware of that links her to the actual drugs, just merely to the case its self. There is of course as yet no laboratory analysis of the contents of the property which the prosecution will allege is cocaine.

In my respectful submission the case against my client is a weak one and bearing in mind her good character her settled, stable background and address I would urge you to consider bail. There is a gentleman in Court who is able to stand as a considerable surety. There is no chance of her committing further offences on bail. Sir, unless I can assist you further, I would submit that this is a proper case where bail may be granted."

The bench retired to consider the application. I was hopeful, my man had been short and to the point. He came over to me and told me that if they were against us that we could take the question of bail to higher courts on appeal. Summer had been taken back down to the cells when the Court retired and there seemed to be a faint glimmer of hope in her eyes. The Court seemed to take an age to come to a decision, but there was a knock and the Clerk told everyone to stand. The Magistrates trooped back in and the judicial silence was unbearable Summer was brought back again. She stood there meekly looking up at the Bench. The Chairman addressed her and said, "We have given this matter a great deal of consideration. We have paid attention to the nature of the charge and we have listened very carefully to what your counsel has said. In all of the circumstances the Court are prepared to grant you bail, on the condition that the sum of £10,000 be paid as a surety. We will also require that you reside at the address which was given to the Court. Take her down.

It's Our Future

She was gone again. I was confused, they'd just given her bail and they'd just taken her down to the cells.

My usher saw that I looked confused and said, "don't worry luvvie, this way," she ushered me out, "your barrister will explain what's going on it's just normal procedure." She smiled and winked at me and then directed her voice to the Magistrates, "Sir the next case is that of the CPS and Jensen."

Her barrister said, "Well that went better than expected, didn't it? If I was you I'd sprint down the High Street to see if you cannot get a bank draft, don't want too much of that cash sloshing about muddying the waters do we? I'll see you outside the Court when you get back be as quick as you can."

I dashed down the High Street, yes it was all falling into place. I wasn't able to get a bank draft and in the end we decided to lodge the cash in Court. I stood in the witness box as surety. The court could have the money as far as I was concerned.

The barrister made a quick, unopposed, successful application for the return of Summers clothing and passport which had been seized by Customs.

Summer left the well of the Court with tears in her eyes. She had the look of someone who's been through an epic event and survived. And why not.

I embraced her as soon as we'd left the air lock of the Court room doors. We had to be back in a weeks time and the legal team suggested that we call into their offices in the mean time to discuss the strategy of the case.

It's Our Future

I had other ideas. We slipped down the High Street, I stopped, looked at Summer, she looked me in the eyes and smiled.

"You're wonderful, an absolute star, so you've done it all no problems?" I asked already knowing the answer.

"It was all so easy, just so easy, those two days in the Police cells well, we've paid for those a million times over. Inspector Grant came to see me this morning, he doesn't have enough to get Campbell this time but he's on to him big style. As soon as they can pin down the South American side of the operation they'll have him ."

"So then, come on and tell me how did it go in Gran Cayman?"

"Fine, just fine. My cousin Nisha had a buyer lined up already. There's a fortune sitting in our offshore account. It'll have to stay there while until Inspector Grant gets over the shock of finding out that both what Customs seized and what I passed to Police in Gran Cayman was just five kilos of pure plain flour."

"So we've got a few months before the dust settles, the case won't get beyond committal proceedings, because then they'll have the gear analysed but as far as Campbell and anyone else is concerned the reason the case will be dropped is that Customs didn't think that it had a realistic prospect of a conviction on the basis of what I told the authorities about not knowing anything about it. Hopefully by then Campbell won't be around. Someone else, will take his place, another Mr Big Enough but at least this time we'll be starting with a clean slate." Summers relief was obvious as the words flowed out.

It's Our Future

I was so proud of her so glad to have her back and wanted to do something to redress the balance.

"Listen, you haven't been partying for the last three or four weeks, come on lets breach your bail for a couple of days," I said pulling her into a travel agents, "no one will know, we don't have to be back until the weekend. James can look after Well Mobbed, I could do with a break from work and Campbell. Basically nothing else really matters apart from you and me."

She smiled with tears sparkling in her big, animated, dark brown eyes and hugged me burying her head in my chest. It was great to have her back. There was only one thing for it, now the was time that we really did justice to a couple of really wild nights in Ibiza.

I work and party in London. One of the most refreshing and enlightening parts of this is listening to the stories of the people I meet. If you've got any party stories, (matters not how big or small) sagas, gossip, laughs, requests, ideas, suggestions, views, bellyaches or gripes about any aspect of clubland please drop me a line and a s.a.e., I'll try to reply to you all.

Enjoy!

A.D. Atkins
P.O.Box. 10583.
London.
SW1V 3ZL